Peppermint

Mocha Murder

A Molly Brewster Mystery

with Killer Recipes

Pam Moll

Peppermint Mocha Murder

Holidays are Murder Series

A Molly Brewster Mystery with Killer Recipes

A Novel by Pam Moll
Copyright ©2018 by Pamela Laux Moll
First paperback edition © March 2018
by Pamela Laux Moll
Printed in the United States of America
www.gopamela.com
ISBN: 978-1-892357-10-6
Beau Ridge Publishing

To my family

ACKNOWLEDGEMENTS

Major thanks are owed to my beta readers and to my editor. You all are a wonderful team. Many thank-yous to all my family and friends for testing the recipes and for their encouragement and support that assisted me through the journey, from the bottom of my heart, thank you. And special thanks to all my readers and Social Media friends, who are very kind and supportive. I truly love writing for you all!

To my husband, Kyle, who stood by me. To my kids; Lissa and Kevin, Ben and Sarah, Courtney, Tyler and Arrie, and Brandon. I love you all!

If you bought your book on Amazon, please leave a review.

Holidays are Murder Series:

A Molly Brewster Mystery

with Killer Recipes

To Do List:

1. *Wrap presents*

2. *Deal with Granny*

3. *Solve a Murder*

Cast of Characters

Molly Brewster – owner of café *Addicted to the Bean*
Deputy Drew "Lucky" Powell – Palma County
Granny Dee McFadden – Molly's grandmother
Nadine McFadden Brewster – Molly's usually absent mother
Aurora Kelly – Barista at the Bean, Molly's friend
Bailey (Bales) Smith – Barista at the Bean
Chris Musk – Hot male, Barista at the Bean
Erica Alltop – Barista at the Bean
Fiona Smith – Barista at the Bean, Erica's mother
Snickers – Molly's sidekick, Chocolate Lab
Henrietta Filadora – Granny Dee's cook
Jet Mitterhammer – Granny's Gardener
Deputy Ted Walker – Police Officer, Palma County
Detective Dawn Lacey – Detective, Palma County
Detective Ted Chandler – Detective, Palma County
Chief O'Donnell – Chief of the Sheriff Department
Jack Doughty – Doughy Delights part owner
Felix Doughty – Doughy Delights owner
Kate Hawkins – Yoga champion
Mayor Clawson – Mayor of Bay Isles
Todd Clawson – Mayor Clawson's son
Duncan Clawson – Mayor Clawson's brother
Mrs. Reynolds – Molly's nosey, next door neighbor
Jim Grinchily Grist – A disappointing Angler
Timothy Carlin – Granny's sometime suitor
Several McFadden Aunts – Molly's usually absent aunties   Plus Lots of elderly Bay Isles denizens – usually always present

I'm a Coffeeholic. On the road to recovery.
Just kidding.
I'm on the road to the coffee shop.
~ Anonymous

CHAPTER ONE

There was nothing I hated more than the smell of burnt coffee. In most places this wouldn't be a big deal, but this was a café, and it created a bit of a panic. It was a few minutes past five a.m., and in less than an hour my first customers of the day would arrive.

Moving past the granite counter in my cozy store, I reflexively pulled my apron embroidered with the words "*A coffee a day keeps the grumpy away*" from the peg. I yanked it over my head, catching it on my frizzy reddish-blond hair. My ginger hair was my mother's family claim, a legacy that skipped her. But Granny Dee had been a redheaded McFadden, though now her mop of hair was mostly gray. I love my mother and Granny to bits, but there were many traits and genes I wish they would have kept to themselves. Fortunately, their baking gene isn't one of them.

I propped the café back door open to draw out the smell. Overhead the dark rose-blue sky held a smattering of stars. The barely audible sounds came from the skittering of egrets and pelicans across the bay.

Undaunted by the interruption in my morning routine, I examined the brown tar-like substance that coated the bottom of the glass pot. With the heating pad left on, the pot had boiled itself dry. Who had forgotten to clean the coffeepot? Did Aurora or Bales close last night? Even as I asked the question to myself, I knew it was ridiculous because both baristas knew better.

At my café, *Addicted to the Bean*, we made umpteen kinds of coffee with almost a dozen different brewing options, from the French press, to pour-overs, to drip, to cold brew and espresso, and turning the equipment off was second nature and burning it was for amateurs.

The lingering aroma of burnt coffee was strong in the front of the café. It might as well have been stinky gym socks or dirty diaper smells welcoming the early morning commuters.

In the small kitchen I ran fresh water, salt, and vinegar in the glass carafe, and then placed it in the deep stainless sink. I scrubbed with a bottlebrush at the gooey sediment on the bottom. While trying to shake it loose, the water splashed and a cloud of burnt grounds spewed in my face. I coughed and sneezed.

"Aw. Peppermint coffee." I sneezed again and again, as I covered my nose and fanned away the fumes me.

"You might know," I muttered to myself, "the one flavor I'm allergic to."

I found it hard to believe we had switched to peppermint flavored beans. It seemed as if we had just been sampling the pumpkin spiced ones. It was 20 days before Christmas and 20 days before my 30th birthday.

Still muttering, I scooped up the glass carafe and placed it on the counter. "Bales or Aurora can deal with this later."

I tilted my head and tried again to remember who had closed. Aurora? Definitely Aurora. Bales had taken off early to pick up her son at soccer practice.

Aurora was my first hire when I opened the café six months earlier, and she loved a soothing cup of peppermint anything. Sometimes I think she brewed it just to watch me sneeze.

She was the youngest person to work at the shop, and probably the youngest living in the town of Bay Isles. At twenty-six, she worked full-time and went to an online college. She lived with her parents on the bay side of the island.

Her dad was a dentist and her mom a yoga teacher at the dance studio three doors down from the Bean. She was the closest person I had to a friend after eight months of living in Bay Isles.

How did I become the energetic owner of a café that also housed a book nook? I moved to the Gulf Coast town of Bay Isles, Florida after I inherited money from my grandfather Lowes McFadden, my mom's dad. The great thing about my business is I get to be around my passion every day. I love books and I love coffee. The bad thing about my business is I'm not a people person. I'm usually grumpy and can't even speak to people until I've had at least one and a half cups of coffee and a blueberry muffin. Then I can smile. But I don't do chit-chat until I've had my second cup of Joe.

The kitchen door squeaked open and my sidekick and loyal chocolate Labrador Retriever, Snickers, stuck his head in. He wrinkled his nose at the smell and cocked his head. I agreed with him. I might only be the owner of the café with less than a year's experience, but even I knew this wasn't how a coffee house should smell.

"Someone forgot to turn off a burner last night," I said to my dog, Snickers.

He tilted his head.

"Yeah, we received peppermint flavored coffee yesterday. I think Aurora forgot to empty the pot."

With the mention of Au-Ror-Ah, Snickers' head perked up. She was his favorite and overindulged him with doggie treats and lots of scratches behind the ears.

Snickers looked at me like *where's breakfast?*

"Hold on." I scooped a large cup of dry dog food into his tin bowl, and before placing it on the tiled floor in the office I dumped a half can of pumpkin into the dry mixture. Snickers salivated and wagged his tail.

"Lucky for you, we still have ten more cans of pumpkin to use up." I smiled at him and patted his head. "Eat up," I said, signaling to my dog that it was okay to eat. He stuck his head into the dish and lapped up the pumpkin coated kibbles.

The large wall clock displayed 5:15 a.m. I always arrived at 5, one hour before the café opened. Each day we began fresh, using cold, unyielding equipment to make warm treats and drinks.

I retrieved today's pastries from the lock box in the alley. The baked goods were delivered earlier by the local pastry shop. We made our own specialties in the café, like our famous gooey butter cake, but for the other treats I relied on the pastry shop ten miles away.

I left the back door propped open to allow delivery people easy access.

As was my routine, I returned to the front of the store and turned on the espresso, drip, smoothie and Chemex machines and started brewing coffee. I marked the brew times on the chart hanging on the wall outside my small office. This reminded us to dump the old batches and start brewing fresh ones. No one liked old bitter coffee.

As I arranged the fresh pastries in the display case, I pulled out the day-old ones, setting them aside in a box. Day-old baked goods never made an encore appearance in my café. Instead, they were handed over to a volunteer that showed up every day from the non-profit community center.

I prepped the sandwich bar and made a note to buy more tomatoes. After filling the half-and-half metal carafes, I brewed more coffee. When I placed the creamers, honey, sugar, cinnamon, nutmeg, mocha dust and several spices on the coffee prep station, I noticed the white napkins stamped with our green logo were low. I refilled them and looked around for the next task.

There were a thousand details to attend to. But I've opened the shop for the past 180 days solo, so everything had become second nature to me.

I poured a cup of coffee, added low-fat milk, sweetener and a smidgeon of cinnamon. Once I settled behind the counter, I opened the register and began to sort the cash. I put down the twenties and started on the tens when I heard a noise coming from the kitchen. I shut the register, zipped the empty bank bag and hid the cash in the flower vase.

Taking my freshly poured coffee with me, I was about to swing open the kitchen door when I heard footsteps. It gave me a chill. Ever so slowly, I opened the door and collided with the pastry delivery truck driver. My hot coffee cascaded down the front of his shirt.

"Ouch!" he yelled, holding his shirt away from his scalded chest.

"Oh my gosh, Felix! I am sooo sorry," I exclaimed, trying to dry him off with my apron.

"No cream and sugar next time," he quipped with a wry smile.

I felt my face burn Christmas red. "I'm so sorry. I didn't hear you sneak in, and you scared the cappuccino out of me!" I quipped back.

Why hadn't he yelled hello? Most of the deliveryman do. Maybe because he was new? He'd only been in Bay Isles a few weeks. His cousin, Jack Doughty, was the eponymous founder of Doughy Delights.

"Sorry, I didn't mean to frighten you," he gasped, still stinging from the warm liquid. "I thought we already received your delivery. I just loaded them in the pastry case." I bustled about looking for paper towels, but only found a handful of napkins. I handed them to him.

"Yes. I did that drop a half hour ago. But when I went back to the bakery, Jack asked me to bring you these freshly baked cupcakes sprinkled with peppermint."

My nose itched when he mentioned peppermint. I handed him another wad of napkins in exchange for the three boxes of cupcakes. My mind raced. *What was the catch? Just being a nice guy?*

Felix who finally managed to not look shocked from the spilled coffee on his shirt, relaxed a bit and looked around. "Does Erica open today?" He asked coyly.

"No, she comes in later this morning."

He nodded as he wiped the coffee stains. "Do you know if she still works part time for her ex?" He asked looking up from the task.

I rubbed my chin. I did know that Erica, one of my baristas, worked another job part-time at the island seafood restaurant, but I didn't know she had an ex-boyfriend. I shrugged.

"I didn't expect that to last," he mumbled.

I wasn't sure if he was referring to Erica's relationship to her ex or her employment status at the restaurant. Since both were a mystery to me, I was about to ask for clarification when the swinging kitchen door crept open.

Snickers, with pumpkin-tinted jowls, came in the kitchen to greet Felix, who leaned over to pet my dog with his free hand, while blotting the coffee off his shirt with the other.

Snickers' long pink tongue made a tour around the exterior of his jowls, cleaning the remains of the pumpkin.

"What's your dog's name again?" Felix asked, seemingly unmindful to the fact that coffee stains dotted his shirt. His dark hair was tousled and windblown. He looked almost like his cousin, except for a growing beard. They both wore the same dark-framed, distinguished glasses and the same wild hair. It made them look like twins, come to think of it. I assumed he was in his late 30s or early 40s, but I was never good at judging the ages of strange men.

"Snickers," I answered.

"Oh." Felix raised an eyebrow.

I automatically added, "Yes, like my favorite candy bar. But if you get to know Snickers, you'll find that he really does snicker at people."

He held out his free hand for Snickers to inspect. It was soon covered in slobbery kisses.

"I'm sorry about that," I said quickly.

"No problem," said Felix, as he wiped the slobber from his hand on the napkin. "Good boy, Snicks."

I smoothed my apron and tucked a loose curl behind my ear. Unlike most of my single girlfriends, I was never the one to fuss about fashion. My time was spent at the café or reading books, not clothes shopping. Maybe an update to my coffee-colored wardrobe was in order.

"There's a restroom down the hall behind the book nook." I was worried about time. I had a fixed schedule each morning and no room for chit chat, plus I still hadn't finished my first cup of Joe.

Felix shook his head. "I'll be fine. I have a spare shirt in the truck." His gaze softened.

"I'm so sorry," I repeated.

"No worries Molly. I should have said something."

"It's Mo."

He arched his eyebrows and looked like he was trying to refrain from saying "oh" again.

"My friends, employees, family ... well, except my mom, call me Mo. Short for Molly." I guess I never had let him know my nickname, nor that my full name was Molly McFadden Brewster.

"Mo? Like the Three Stooges?" Felix said with a cheerful smile.

I liked the small gap in his front teeth and decided he had a nice smile.

"I get that a lot. And no jokes about Mo sells Jo," I said, smiling back.

Felix chuckled. "I do love a good joke, but not at someone else's expense. We get enough cop jokes at the doughnut shop."

I nodded and glanced at my watch. Snickers had made his way back to the front of the shop, anxious to be let outside after his breakfast.

I peaked at the cupcakes. "Oh, gorgeous!" And they were, pure sweet perfection, which could have only been improved by omitting the peppermint sprinkles.

"Jack wanted me to give them to you. No charge. And no hard feelings, he said to tell you."

I narrowed my eyes. *Hard feelings? What was I missing?*

Felix stood there expecting a reply. When I stayed silent, he added, "He said you'd know what he meant."

I had no idea what Jack meant.

"Would you like a coffee to go? I mean besides the one on your shirt?"

"Sure, thanks."

"What do you drink?"

"Regular coffee, black."

"Black, I think that fits you."

"Why's that?" He smiled.

"From what I know of you. I'd say you're a minimal-fuss, no-nonsense kind-of-a guy. Right? During my 6 months running the Bean I've been observing the coffee habits of the citizens of Bay Isles. It's a game I like to play when someone orders a beverage."

"Hah, you mean like psychological profiling?"

"Well, more like java profiling."

Felix looked at his shirt, "In that case, what do you drink and what does it tell about you?"

I laughed, pointing to his shirt "That's a regular coffee with sweetener and low-fat milk and a smidgeon of cinnamon."

I'm somewhat of a dual personality. Sometimes I have it all together while other times I enjoy cutting loose and being spontaneous. Cream and sugar, well based on what I see of my customers that's usually a sign of being logical and creative."

"Couldn't it be a sign they want to mask the flavor of the coffee?"

I laughed. "Well, it's far from an exact science."

Snickers barked at the front door, causing both of us to look his way.

"I better let you get back to your job. I'll take a raincheck on the coffee."

"Okay then. Tell Jack thanks for the cupcakes. We'll make good use of these."

Felix lingered for a few more seconds fussing over his shirt. On his way out he said, "The cupcakes are gluten free!"

"No kidding," I said over my shoulder as he left through the back door. It wasn't the gluten that would get to me, it was the peppermint sprinkles.

The start of this day had been full of odd surprises.

Within a half hour, the money was moved from the flower vase to the cash register, water gurgled and dripped, and kettles chirped. The creams chilled in their places. The aroma of freshly baked muffins, scones, and Granny Dee's specialty—gooey butter cake—dwarfed the burnt coffee smell.

I had just completed my opening routine, when I heard Snickers barking at the back door.

"Felix, did you forget something?" I yelled as I swung open the kitchen door.

The kitchen was empty. Snickers was staring out back.

"What's up boy?" I said to my dog, as I walked slowly over to the door that was slightly ajar and peered out.

A beautiful cat with deep ocean blue eyes stared up at me.

"Poor thing. This is the third time this week I've seen you hanging around the café," I said softly not wanting to frighten the cat away.

The stray cat leaped to the pastry lockbox. He was sniffing intently, with his whiskers back and his nose twitching up and down like mine did when I smelled peppermint. He was sleek, much thinner than George, Granny's cat, and his once dark-tipped creamy coat looked dull.

"Are you hungry?"

The cat dug his claws at the crumbs on the metal pastry box. Then it rolled over and licked the dark brown fur on his stomach.

"Stay and no bark," I commanded Snickers. "You too," I said to the cat not sure cats could understand commands.

I retreated to the kitchen to prepare something to feed the beautiful stray. "Hmmm, what have I got for it to eat?" I said rubbing my chin.

I put some pieces of cheese on a plate and opened a can of tuna I had been saving for a quick lunch snack. Then I filled a small bowl of water.

When I returned to the back porch, the cat was still perched on top of the pastry box. I placed the plate of food and the water bowl outside the door and moved back slowly.

The cat eyed me and Snickers, then jumped down to sniff the food. While the stray pawed at the food, I noticed coffee grounds clinging to his fur. Within seconds the cat with his back slightly arched was hungrily wolfing down the food while keeping a fearful eye glued on me and Snickers.

Snickers wagged his tail, as if to say, *go for it.*

Strays and lost cats always made me feel a little sad. This one looked like he could be a poster cat for a humane society ad. He was probably once a beautiful Siamese cat.

The two times before, when I had seen the cat, I tried to lure him with a plate of food, but I had finally left the plate on the back boardwalk near my porch for him to eat in his own good time. When I had returned later the food was gone. This was the first time the stray ate while Snickers and I watched on.

I would call the sheriff's office later today about the stray. I hated to think someone had lost a pet.

"Let's go Snickers. Let's leave –," I wondered what to call him or her, "– let's leave Kona alone." The mocha colored stray cat with coffee grounds on his head looked up at me and meowed. I wondered if it was cat talk for 'thank you.'

I returned to the front of the café and moved back the lacy beige curtains and propped the front door open. The red velvet bows I'd pinned to the wreath whirled and danced in the slight bay breezes. I placed the chalkboard easel outside with its display of three chalked handwritten lines:

PEPPERMINT MOCHA MURDER

Brew of the Day: Java Jampit good acidity, heavy body.

Fresh roasted beans by the bag.
Gluten-Free Peppermint Mocha Cupcakes.

Every morning I opened the door, and every morning a sense of pride bubbled up inside me.

The weather in Bay Isles this morning was absolutely perfect. It was past hurricane season and the holidays were in full swing. I still found it hard, after living here for less than a year, for it to be warm during the winter months. Even so, my café was slammed each morning no matter what the temperature was outside.

I refilled the water bowl outside perched under a small sign that proclaimed; *Dog Parking.* Snickers took interest in the post where the bowl sat. He sniffed and sniffed. Obviously, this location was his spot and a place to gather info on other dogs—the canine version of a newspaper. Snicks hesitated before reluctantly following me back in the café.

My first customer showed up in tandem with my first-shift employee, Bales.

Coffee in hand, grown-up pants on, shine in my eyes, smile on my face—yup, I was ready for the day to begin.

Behind every successful person is a
substantial amount of coffee.
~ Anonymous

CHAPTER TWO

"The perfect cup of coffee is mystifying," Bailey, or Bales as we called her, commented. She tugged on her apron and smoothed the front pocket. With precision she clipped her name tag on the strap, above the *Save the Manatees* pin.

"Someone left the carafe on the sideboard burner on all night," I said. "There's nothing mystifying about that."

"I bet that was some wicked coffee," Aurora said, "but I'm sorry to hear that." She frowned and poked a wooden spoon into a bowl of yellow gooey butter batter.

I sighed. Typical that neither one of my baristas would disclose who did the crime. It was like watching two siblings protect one another.

"I guess it's my fault since I closed." Aurora finally admitted being the culprit. "I placed the peppermint coffee on the antique sideboard, but in a rush to leave the café, I must

18

have forgotten whether I left it on or off." Aurora's lush red lips, and dark-eyed make-up almost gave her a cat-like appearance. Her apron read, *KISS ME I'M ITALIAN*.

"I should have reminded you about the coffee samples," Bales said to Aurora and frowned slightly.

I shook my head.

"Sorry boss," they chimed in unison. Both Aurora and Bales giggled at their responses.

I shook my head again and then faked a big sneeze.

Aurora burst into laughter and Bales succumbed with her.

When they settled down, Aurora said, "Sorry to put you in a rush this morning and sorry about the peppermint too."

"I'll get over it."

I walked over to the cooling muffins sitting on the counter and inhaled. "One of your blueberry muffins will help."

Aurora laughed, as she handed me a freshly baked muffin.

I split the warm muffin open and the fragrant steam rose from the center. When I took my first bite, I closed my eyes and sighed. "Oh my," I mumbled as I crammed more of the muffin in my mouth. "Amazing Aurora, this is the best moment of my week."

Aurora shook her head. "You need to get out more."

Like her fresh baked good, Aurora was amazing. She was a genuine person with a sense of humor, and I could tell during her interview that we'd be great friends. She was always chatting with the customers, wore a smile every day, and was a comic. She was punctual and never had a bad day, and sported short black cropped hair spiked with mousse. Her ears sparkled with four earrings in each ear. She was a music fanatic and a fervent force to be reckoned with if you got on her bad side. She knew what she wanted and how to get it. At the moment, she was saving every penny to open her own bakery. Aurora was one helluva baker.

Bales, on the other hand, was a passionate and self-assured woman who shared her opinions often. She had no time for foolishness and believed in many Save-the-Earth and environmental-worthy causes. Similar to Aurora, she wore her no-nonsense auburn hair slightly spiked and her hazel eyes sparkled under her purple plaid reading glasses. Bales once told me she had 20/20 vision and wore different designer glasses every day to make her appear smarter and more sophisticated. She was 35 years old, divorced and had a six-year-old son, but looked and acted 65, even without the glasses. She'd be just as content to sit in a rocker knitting a scarf and exchanging casserole recipes.

"Are we off the hook?" Aurora asked.

"Seriously, I appreciate the apologies. I really don't care who did it, we just need to be more careful. I don't want to wake up one morning to a four-alarm fire. Capiche?"

Both employees dutifully nodded.

This morning, 50 percent of my crew were in the coffee shop. The other three and a half employees would be in before noon for a meeting and to help decorate for the Holly Fest. Chris was our only male employee. Erica was a young, flirtatious part-timer. Bales's mother Fiona was a full-timer. And Granny Dee was half of an employee because she didn't get paid and liked to think she worked at the Bean.

Her extra pair of hands came in handy, especially when elbow deep in flour. She made the tenderest pie crusts. I called this zany collection of staff the *alphabet crew*. Ironically, everyone that worked at the Bean, except for me, had names that started with the first seven letters of the alphabet.

For this morning's rush, Aurora and Bales seemed ready to go. Granny showed up a few hours every day to sweep, wipe, mop, wash, scrub, and bake—and, of course, turn out those delicious pie crusts. She disliked coffee and only sipped our imported teas. It wasn't that she didn't like the taste of a fine roasted bean … it was her fear of getting herself addicted to drinking it. She said she didn't want to make herself vulnerable.

The café door was still propped open and I saw a familiar face peep around it.

I hustled out of the kitchen and over to greet her.

"Welcome," I said loud enough to be heard over my other customers. "Welcome, Mrs. Haskell, isn't it?" A woman stood smiling while she looked at the pastry case.

Ms. Haskell drinks a mixture of lemonade and tea with fresh mint. A Diet Coke of the tea world. She's mid-fifty-something, doesn't look a day over forty, if that, and thin as a rail.

"Molly dear," Ms. Haskell said, "please call me Kate."

"What will it be today, *Kate*? A piece of gooey butter cake or a spinach ricotta croissant?"

Kate Haskell, was wearing skintight navy yoga pants that looked air-brushed on, a pale-pink tank top, and her highlighted blonde hair was tied back with a shocking pink hair tie to match her bazooka pink tennis shoes.

"No, let's go with one of those peppermint cupcakes today. I'm feeling festive."

"And you should. Only 10 days until the Holly Fest." I handed her a plate with the pink iced cupcake and glass of our signature Arnold Palmer, an iced tea with freshly squeezed lemon juice and simple syrup. Kate Haskell didn't drink coffee, but thankfully that never kept her from stopping at the Bean after her yoga class.

"Do you have fresh mint?" She handed me her debit card.

As I ran her card, Aurora came over and handed Kate a napkin which held a few sprigs of fresh mint.

"Did you know Molly grows the mint? And other spices like oregano, thyme, dill, rosemary, lemongrass and a dozen different mint flavors," Aurora said with a faint, mischievous smile.

"Not now," I murmured softly under my breath to Aurora, who ignored me.

Kate looked at Aurora, an amused and indulge-me smile on her coral painted lips. "No, I didn't realize that." She picked up one sprig, stared at it, and then plunked it in her glass.

"She has an amazing green thumb," Aurora beamed. "She even sells her spices to other shops around the state, like the Thyme for

Tea café, Lavender and Lace High Tea, Hidden Treasure Tearoom, and several spice stores. We ship her spices and mints all over."

Kate stared at the second sprig on the napkin like it was a celebrity.

"Well, I hadn't realized you were a baker, café owner, and a spice gardener too. Don't you live in one of the apartments in this complex?" She asked, puzzled.

I nodded. "I do. I keep my gardens at my grandmother's place. She has a lot of land for my gardening hobby."

"And Molly's allergic to mint, right boss?" Aurora shared.

Oh Geez, why did Aurora have to go tell her that?

Kate held the tea glass midair under her nose before pursing her lips and taking a dubious swallow. She tilted her head and raised her eyebrows. "Allergic?"

I wasn't proud of this odd allergy. And I could have easily gone without sharing this. I glared at Aurora and turned and smiled at Kate.

"Well, it's peppermint more than anything. It's not like I'll go into anaphylactic shock. It's more a sneezing, coughing allergy thing."

"Like hay fever," Kate said. "Were you tested?"

I shook my head. "I didn't realize it until I played a role as a reporter for our campus weekly Internet show at my university one semester. I kept wheezing when I interviewed people, only to find out they had eaten Tic Tac mints from the green room before the interviews. And their proximity, and sharing a microphone with me, made me sneeze."

"No kidding." Kate tilted her head to one side like an inquisitive puppy and then giggled like a little girl, and to my embarrassment, Bales and Aurora felt an irrepressible need to join in.

"You ladies are incorrigible," I said feigning embarrassment and fighting the urge to giggle too.

"How do you brush your teeth?" Kate asked, now clearly intrigued.

"Ironically, I never cared for mint-flavored toothpaste. So that was never an issue. And when I garden I wear a pollen mask and rubber gloves. We also have a helper at Granny Dee's place, Jet. He's a gardener slash handyman."

"Jetson Mitterhammer?" Kate's smile faded, and she looked at me with surprise.

Aurora glanced from me to Kate and back again, suddenly interested in the connection between Granny's gardener and this petite lady. I was too.

"I don't know Jet's last name, but how many Jets are there in Bay Isles? Do you know him?" I hardly knew Granny's gardener. I was still getting to know my regular customers, and the other Bay Isles' Village shopkeepers and didn't spend a lot of time at Granny's. When I did visit, it was to garden, rummage through her attic for vintage clothes, or enjoy Sunday dinners, and Jet wasn't usually there.

Kate Haskell raised an eyebrow and took a few seconds to reply. "We hang out in the same circles occasionally. I met him at the newcomer's lunch." She chuckled. "I just moved here last year."

Aurora's mirthful dark eyes and normally placid face had taken on a curious look. Usually she was the picture of high enthusiasm enhanced by her good humor, but now she became a quiet observer, leaving me to pry by myself.

Fortunately, I already had my second cup of coffee. I'd be good at prying now. And I was curious, since I wondered where Kate and Granny's gardener hung out.

"Did you know Jet before you moved here?" I asked, wondering if Kate was married. I stole a quick look at her left hand. No wedding ring. Maybe she and Granny's gardener had dated. They appeared to be about the same age.

I ask a lot of questions. I possessed a nimble mind that burned with curiosity. The kind of curiosity that could kill the proverbial cat.

Our conversation was disrupted by loud children's voices that suddenly filled the café. Two of the Carlin's numerous granddaughters—there are more than I've been able to count—came to the counter to order hot chocolate and cookies. Their grandfather, Timothy, strolled in the front door behind them.

At the same time, the kitchen door swung open and Granny Dee teetered in with a tray containing colorfully decorated sugar cookies. Once again, she had snuck in through the back door. Didn't the McFadden's ever use the front door? Her timing was impeccable. Or was it? I wondered how she conjured up these deliciously decorated goodies in time to feed the Carlin grandkids.

Was it my imagination, or did Kate scamper for safety when she saw my grandmother? My baristas also seemed to take refuge behind the large cypress paneled shelves in the nook, both pretending to straighten rows of books.

"Timothy, so good to see you." Granny Dee's raspy voice carried a distinct aura and a genuine thrill to see him.

PAM MOLL

My granny thrilled to see anyone? I stared in surprise at her, wrapped in a gray skirt that swirled around her ankles. *A skirt?* I wanted to question her outfit choice, but my mother had raised me right, and I couldn't utter a word except to say, "Hi Grandma."

I have measured out my life
with coffee spoons.
~ T.S. Eliot

CHAPTER THREE

"Edith!" exclaimed Timothy Carlin, as he pushed his way past his granddaughters.

Granny Dee stopped abruptly and stared googly-eyed at Timothy.

From out of nowhere, Chris appeared from the kitchen wiping seemingly invisible specks of coffee grounds from the inside of a glass carafe.

Granny Dee turned in surprise and her tray of cookies collided with Chris. A loud crash echoed as glass hit the tiled floor, but Granny's startled shriek was louder.

Silence followed.

All at once everyone started talking.

"Why'd you come barging in?" Granny demanded.

"What are you doing standing in the doorway?" Chris replied.

"Humph," Granny sniffled. I was impressed she still balanced the plate of cookies upright, considering she could be quite clumsy without her cane.

"Careless, sloppy baristas," she mumbled.

"Here, let me take those cookies," I offered, guiding Granny gingerly away from the door. I grabbed the tray.

Granny waved her hand. "Whatever. I'm just ..."

I held up a hand to stop her from berating my employee in front of customers. Sometimes I just had to take a stand. Even against Granny.

"Granny, have a seat and get out of the kitchen doorway. Chris, get a broom and clean up that mess." I calculated quickly that our second glass carafe had been destroyed today, and it wasn't even noon yet.

"Aurora and Bales, please get Mr. Carlin and his lovely granddaughters their breakfast and refill Kate's mint Arnold Palmer."

Was I imagining it, or did Granny scowl?

Chris swooped in from the kitchen holding a broom and dustpan. Granny paid no attention to the task, until she saw him start to sweep.

"Here, let me you clumsy dunce. You won't get it all." She grabbed the broom. *There's the granny I love– taking control.* I knew it was a form of an apology for scolding at my employees.

PEPPERMINT MOCHA MURDER

Granny Dee loved drinking hot tea. She ruled the roost with a sharp tongue, whined about the cooler mornings while clutching a steaming cup in both hands, and at night she could be found watching re-runs of Murder She Wrote, anything on the Hallmark Channel or reading Agatha Christie novels.

I admired my Granny, a.k.a. Edith D. McFadden. She was a tough cookie and quite grumpy. 79 years young, she'd turn 80 several weeks before I turned 30. She could be hard, sarcastic and mean-spirited, and her face was often scrunched up like she was eating something sour. She talked tough for such a tiny old woman, but deep down she was all about family. We McFadden's stuck together. Technically I was a Brewster, my father's surname, but having been raised by my mother and all my aunts, I often thought of changing it to McFadden. The name definitely matched my ginger hair which crowned McFadden heads for generations.

Although Granny could be tough sometimes, she was a good helper around the café and would lay her life down for any of us. A former nurse, she liked to give advice on all things related to medical situations. Granny adored her family, even if she didn't show it and she harassed me constantly about finding a man.

"Mo, your biological clock is running out," she declared, as if I was a spaceship zooming to earth, and when the clock stopped, BOOM!

I rarely thought about settling down and having a family. I was doing quite well, thank you very much. At 29, I was broke, single, owned a café, partially working on a PhD, and living in an apartment above the café that I owned. Not too bad.

"It could be worse, Granny Dee," I always replied. "I could be 29, broke, single, back in school, unemployed, and living with you."

Yes, that was me a year ago. Indeed, I had lived with Granny Dee and loved her big house, but her grumpy attitude was a challenge.

Today I lived in one of the rented apartments above the shopping village where my café was located. I was a flight of stairs and 182 weather-beaten boardwalk steps from my work, and less than 100 steps to a manicure and a haircut, which I indulged in once a month. A dry cleaner, dentist, yoga studio (which I never participated in), and a sub shop and Gator Joe's Bait and Tackle were also within walking distance. My favorite place in the Villages of Bay Isles was the guitar shop. Even though I don't play the guitar, Snickers and I have been known to sit and listen to the guitarists while reading Agatha Christie.

For the next 30 minutes or so, the Bean was back to business. Customers came and went. Fresh coffee brewed. My staff tended to customers and daily chores. Granny was situated outside speaking with Mr. Carlin and thrusting her secret weapon—sweets—on him and his granddaughters.

For the hundredth time, I felt a huge swell of gratitude to my grandfather.

Leave it to my granddaddy Lowes to be sensible. If he had left me money with no stipulations, he knew I'd have used it to pay off my college loans or go on a cruise to some exotic place or buy a new car. But instead, his Will stipulated I use the money to open a business. I also received money to set up a household in Bay Isles.

Thank you granddaddy. He had been smart and wanted to keep me close to Granny Dee, but not underfoot. So, I rented one of the apartments in the building behind and upstairs from the café.

One of the many perks of living in our village was that we're located on a barrier island that's barely five miles long and three miles wide, so I could ride a bike or take a golf cart or a boat to get to where I needed to be. A drawbridge connected the Village of Bay Isles to the mainland. Most of the area we lived was bordered by the

Gulf of Mexico, Tampa Bay, and various inlets. It was truly an ideal setting for my business.

I joke around a lot about not being a people person, but in reality, I love dealing with all sorts of people.

I figured if I could grow up in a household with only my mom and an older brother, and no father since I was ten, then I could survive living close to Granny.

Suddenly, Snickers dashed toward the front door, skittering on the tile. He only greeted a few customers this way. And without looking outside, I knew Deputy Lucky was in the vicinity.

Two Palma County Sheriff's Deputies walked in, dressed in tan uniforms and mirrored Costa sunglasses that hid their eyes. Sidearms always hung from their waists. At other businesses, the cops showing up meant trouble was afoot. But here, I knew them as two large lattes and a blueberry muffin and a biscotti. Deputy Drew "Lucky" Powell ate the blueberry muffin (a man after my heart) and Deputy Ted Walker the biscotti.

Actually, I got the idea about analyzing people by the type of coffee they drink the first time Deputy Drew Powell walked into the Bean. I call him Deputy Handsome.

It struck me as I handed him his morning latte that he saw it as just one of those small comforts that makes life truly worth living. And maybe he liked it because it took the bitterness out of the coffee, just like he wanted to take the bitterness out of life by serving and protecting the community.

So, what started out as a little fun, fantasizing about the kind of person he was, well, turned into a habit.

I smiled. I hadn't seen Deputy Lucky in a few weeks. For reasons unknown to the residents of Bay Isles, Deputy Drew Powell had been nicknamed Lucky. I thought I heard it had something to do with their weekly fishing trips, but I'm positive it had to do with his uncanny apprehension of criminals.

Our community of Bay Isles didn't have its own police department, and instead residents were protected by the Palma County Sheriff's office. Crime overall in Bay Isles was relegated to thefts, robberies and assaults. Deputy "Lucky" Drew had more arrests than half the department. Granted, he had a zero-tolerance rule, but his arrests tended to fall on the lesser offenses.

"Hey guys," I said with a slight sexy twang, wondering where in the world it came from. *Have I been hanging around Erica too much?* Erica, one of my part-time workers was quite the flirt.

"The usual?" I asked, and managed to shake the twang loose, flashing the deputies my biggest smile. I was on my third cup of coffee, and it showed.

"Hi Mo. Yes please, lattes," Deputy Lucky
said, while Deputy Ted was bent over petting Snickers.

While I made their drink order, Aurora gathered their pastries.

Lucky smiled warmly at me while I worked. He was a handsome guy with a pale complexion that tanned easily, large attractive green eyes, dimples, and pearly white teeth. He wore his sandy-colored hair cropped short and had the most distinguished walk I'd ever seen. He sauntered on a six-foot thin, but muscular, frame. If I was looking to date someone, which I wasn't, Lucky was my kind of guy. He was around my age too.

The deputies stopped at the Bean a few times a week. Lucky claimed they were addicted to my flavor-of-month lattes and came by for their fix on their way north to Bridgeport Falls, where the Palma County Sheriff precinct was headquartered. I'd like to think that Deputy Lucky enjoyed seeing my smiling face over a perfect cup of coffee, but that was my ego dreaming. Lucky's partner, Ted Walker, was a distinguished mid-50s veteran.

He asked, pointing in the case, "Are those peppermint cupcakes?"

"They are," I replied. "Would you like one? On the house." I grinned.

"How can I say no to a free peppermint cupcake?" Deputy Ted said, grinning.

"Trust me, you can't," I replied.

"Did you make them?" Deputy Lucky asked.

"No, they're from Doughy Doughnut Delights— Jack's place over in Bridgeport Falls," Aurora answered, passing over the pastries on a porcelain plate, and adding two cupcakes.

"Oh, yes, close to our precinct," commented
Deputy Ted, directing his gaze at me.

I handed the lattes to Aurora, who gave them to the two deputies.

"Have you met Felix, Jack's cousin?" I asked, reminded of our hot collision earlier this morning. Something about the second delivery still bothered me.

Deputy Ted looked ready to spit peppermint sprinkles at me. He clutched his latte, frowned, and nodded.

Lucky didn't look my way, but said, "I know him. Do you?"

"Yes. He delivered the pastries this morning," I said from my spot behind the counter.

Lucky gave a nod to his partner and ran a hand through his wavy cropped hair, looking somewhat troubled.

"Hey, before I forget, there's a Siamese cat that's been hanging around back a few times this week."

"A stray?" Deputy Lucky took a sip of his latte.

"Possibly, or a lost pet."

"We haven't had any reports of a lost cat, but we'll let you know if we do. We often find strays in Fort DeSoto Park. Boaters or campers leave them behind."

"That's terrible." My thoughts were on the stray I had named Kona when the bells on the front door jangled. I put on my greet-the-customer face.

A group of fishermen entered.

Amongst the group was Todd Clawson, son of the Bay Isles Mayor. Todd, a handsome eternal college kid, shot a smile at Aurora.

Aurora couldn't hide the little blush on her cheeks. I knew her too well. She was smitten. The very look that set off my radar roped in Aurora every time he flashed his picture-perfect smile. Why couldn't she, and Bales for that matter, tell the difference between a nice guy who was interested and a guy who preyed on pretty girls? *Sort of like me and Snickers candy bars after I go off my diet,* I thought.

Their voices floated over the room, "Jim was ahead of us from the first cast," Todd said.

"He was swinging those fish in the boat before we could bait our hooks," said someone else.

"Yah, every scorable fish counts, but Jim's unfair," the tallest of the anglers added. He stopped speaking when he saw the deputies.

"Hey boys," Deputy Ted said to the group.

"Good day, officer," a few responded.

They stepped aside and let the officers by. I wished I could have spoken with Deputy Lucky a while longer, but we needed all hands-on deck.

I recognized the group and especially the grungiest one, because whenever this particular fisherman came in the café, he was always in a foul mood. If there was a picture in the definition of grumpy in the dictionary, his face would be there. He even trumped Granny. I made a mental note to try and wait on him every time he came in to spare my staff his wrath. He was one of those impossible types of customers who had a snotty comment for everyone in the café. He just barely gave Kate Haskell a look, and she took off out the front door.

The tall one, with mysterious dark eyes but a bright friendly smile, offered to pay for the other two fishermen. "I caught the least amount," he said.

Todd, the mayor's son, tried to refuse, but the other one insisted.

Todd's a caramel double whip latte drinker. He often tells friends how much of a coffee expert he is, rating cafes across South Florida harsher than Gordon Ramsay. He should do everyone a favor and just get a milkshake.

As the grungy fisherman grabbed his extra-large black coffee, he eyed Aurora up and down and muttered a comment. Aurora ignored him and seemed to be biting her tongue. She continued making the other two fishermen's drinks. Mr. Grungy Grumpy looked disgusted as he ate a free sample of Granny's award-winning gooey butter cake. He made a rude comment, something to the effect that it was decent, but not winning any prizes at the county fair.

It doesn't take a psychologist or his coffee choice to see that he's trouble.

Aurora leaned over to me. "I know he's a customer and all and I shouldn't say anything. But when he comes in the café, it's like he's sucked all the sunshine out of the room," whispered Aurora.

"I agree. With his attitude, maybe I should banish him from the café forever." I whispered back to Aurora. He sure got on everyone's nerves and how dare him insult my employees and our food.

Deputies Lucky and Ted said their goodbyes, and I spied them whispering and glancing at Mr. Grumpy before they left. I was busy dashing around assisting the group of fishermen but managed to wave and say goodbye to the officers.

Several of the customers had drifted to the book nook, and two of the fisherman chose a table nearest the kitchen.

Mr. Grumpy didn't bother to thank the other fisherman for paying and walked outside to smoke a cigarette. Snickers wagged his tail at him and the fisherman shooed him away.

Snickers returned the snub with a bark directed at the fisherman as he walked away.

"My sentiments, exactly," I said. I've rarely forbidden a customer from the café, but he deserved to be added to the do-not-enter list.

I spotted Erica in her brightly colored gypsy dress heading in the front door. Her long auburn hair was pinned up in a bun and her pink floral dress billowed in the light breeze. The grumpy fisherman stopped her.

As I glanced at Erica and the fisherman, I caught a flicker of something in her face.

Mr. Grumpy glowered. Erica wore a stubborn look. I've never seen Erica raise her voice, but she looked upset. Her face was flushed.

I read her lips and all I could get was she mentioned something about money. *Money?*

They turned their backs to me.

Within minutes, they were having an all-out argument in the parking lot. I looked around to see if any of my baristas or the other customers noticed.

Everyone seemed to be otherwise engaged. I wondered if I should intervene. *Of course, I shouldn't, but I certainly am,* I decided. My employees are like my family.

It was settled. I decided to sweep the outside porch and eavesdrop. If Erica needed help, I'd be there. I grabbed a broom, but Mr. Grungy had disappeared like a ghost. I was shocked to see a look of terror on Erica's face.

She entered the café and mechanically tied on her green gingham apron. I was concerned as she wandered slowly behind the counter.

Erica blinked at me and looked preoccupied. She jumped when I asked, "Are you okay?"

"I'm fine," she said. Her eyes, however, were scanning the parking lot. She seemed on edge. "I'm just tired."

"Do you need the afternoon off?"

"Huh?" Erica was still staring out the window.

"You seem in another world. Is everything okay?"

She nodded but looked very uncomfortable. "I'm just upset over a horrible person."

Coffee helps me maintain my "never killed anyone streak." ~ Anonymous.

CHAPTER FOUR

It had been a long day at the Bean. The customers had come in a constant stream throughout the day. Despite the broken carafes, the day had been profitable, and I was pleased.

I glanced over at the book nook. There were a plethora of colorful canes and walkers lined up against the wall. Some of the canes had been decorated in green and red, and one especially stood out. It had been wrapped like a candy cane. I didn't realize until I moved to Bay Isles that walking canes were a fashion statement.

I moved past the island's reading group and said my hellos, and then went to grab my backpack from the office. I stopped to review the schedule. On the sheet pinned to the cork board above my desk, I ran my fingers over the names listed; Aurora, Bales, Chris, Granny Dee, (I did schedule her once a week at our slowest time), Erica and Fiona. Erica's mother, Fiona, was on a cruise and wouldn't return until a few days before the Christmas parade and annual Holly Fest event. Like last night, Aurora was scheduled to close. I smiled at the thought of a day off tomorrow. I would miss my team. The whole group was a quirky, special bunch, but they were my family.

I said my goodbyes and left the coffee shop around six-thirty.

I strolled along the village boardwalk toward my apartment situated in the last building. As I looked around the sleepy village, I hoped that nothing would happen to change the sweet ambiance of our quaint little town. It was like a timeless postcard, and I wanted it to stay that way.

The newspaper machine I passed every day still held the free local paper. I pulled open the door and removed the Bay Isles Beach Beacon. By the glow of the street light, I saw on the first page a story about the manatees beginning their annual migration to warmer water. Flipping the pages, I read that Sarah Rosling had delivered her baby girl on Tuesday; Mary Dedham's strawberry pie won first place in the Palma County bake off; and Jim Grist had caught a beast of a fish in the Palma Fishing tournament. Sarah and Mary were regulars at the café. And Jim's photo hoisting the fish looked familiar to me too.

At closer inspection, I knew the winner of the monster fish. Standing next to a Goliath grouper hanging upside down from a hook was

Jim Grist, the grungy fisherman. I immediately thought about Erica and worried that Jim had been the horrible person she mentioned who had upset her. I had sent her home early because she was so shaken up.

Now I could put a name with the face. One of the things I pride myself to try and do as an owner of a local café is to know everyone's names. My café served up coffee, pastries and plenty of gossip. But it had been so crowded this morning, I didn't get to confront Jim, the fisherman of a colossal fish, with a colossal attitude to match.

As I walked back to my apartment, connected to the village, I stared up the street that looked like a Thomas Kinkade oceanside painting. I passed the Yoga studio where Aurora's mom worked, and the Bay Isles' Real Estate office, both closed. Fresh flowers bloomed from the colorful pots resting along the sidewalk. I turned toward the bay and main canal that led to the Gulf. The smell of sea salt and burgers from one of the few island restaurants filled the air. I could travel in any direction from our quaint shopping village and end up at the water.

The sun had set an hour earlier, and the street lamps gave off a soft glow. Snickers let out a low growl as we moved closer to the corner where I was about to turn. I pulled his leash tighter.

Staying close to the side of the building, I peered ahead into the murky darkness. The faint crunch of footsteps came from the breezeway between my building and Gator Joe's Bait and Tackle Shop about ten yards in front of us. I slowed down and slipped back from the shop walkway and thought about my choices. If I let Snickers off the leash he would walk ahead of me and surprise anyone or any animal lurking in the breezeway and could possibly scare them to death. Or I could ignore my over-active imagination and continue my walk. I heard the crunchy noise again and this triggered a bit of uneasiness and I felt fear starting to percolate. Plan of action decided, I bent down and unhooked Snickers leash from his collar.

He surprised me and the stray Siamese cat when he dashed to the end of the boardwalk and barked at the Bait Shop window box.

Through the shadowy light I could see Snickers barking up at a stray cat, possibly Kona. Suddenly, the cat sprang from the window and landed on the head of a man that appeared from out of the breezeway.

I heard the man let out a low-pitched yell. "What in God's name?"

I rushed to the corner and a moment of confusion swept over me and the situation, when

I spotted something perched on top of Deputy Lucky's head.

"Leash your dog, so I can get this wild critter off my head," Deputy Lucky roared as he stepped toward the wall.

"Down," I yelled.

"I don't think raccoons follow the same commands as dogs."

"I wasn't talking to the ca –," I paused and inspected the animal on Lucky's head. "I wasn't talking to the raccoon. I was telling Snickers to back off and stand down."

Snickers immediately lay down at our feet.

A beam of light struck me and blinded my vision for a few seconds. It was directed first at me then Snickers. Lucky flashed the light at the raccoon, but as long as Snickers was underfoot, the raccoon must have decided Lucky's head was a safer choice.

Lucky fixed his gaze on me. I could see two black clawed hands digging into his scalp and tiny droplets of blood trickling from under them and his face starting to redden.

"Snickers come," I said as I ran into the street and away from Deputy Lucky and his raccoon hat.

Lucky smacked the flashlight against the creature and it twisted down his long pant leg like a stripper on a pole. Once it hit the ground it took off in a run.

I sucked in my breath and stepped slowly back to the boardwalk.

"I have to tell you, since I've lived here in South Florida. I've feared alligators, pythons, panthers, black bears and that's just around Granny's backyard. In the water, I fear stingrays, sharks and jellyfish. But a girl shouldn't have to worry about being attacked by a masked animal, unless it's a human, while walking home from work."

Lucky wiped his forehead with his fingers. "Mo, I'm the one that was attacked, because your dog wasn't on a leash." He gave me an exasperated look.

Oops. "Look I'm sorry Deputy Lucky," I said as I pulled a napkin from my backpack and attempted to wipe the scratches on his forehead.

His hand caught mine and he pulled it away. He took the napkin and pressed it against one of the scratches. "You know it's a misdemeanor to have your dog off a leash."

"I had Snickers off the leash because I heard you in the alley. And since when is it against the law?"

"It's unlawful for the owner, possessor or person who keeps any dog to permit the same to run at large," Lucky said it a stern voice.

"Snickers wasn't running *at large* I was with him."

"And if the owner is present but the dog is not controlled through use of a leash, cord, chain–."

"Okay, I get it. I said I'm sorry."

He pulled out a pad of tickets and I felt my face reddened. "You're writing me a ticket?"

He must have seen my eyes widened and my jaw drop, because he smiled. Then he handed me the piece of paper. "Next time you're worried about walking home you can call me or Deputy Walker at this number."

"Really, I wasn't worried until I heard the noise."

"What noise?" His grin faded.

"The alley where you came from."

"I heard it too, and I was investigating. I only spotted Ted Clawson carrying a fishing pole."

I nodded. "I walk through here twice a day and really there's nothing I should be worried about." The mental image of a giant leaping raccoon and Deputy Lucky's scratched head flashed through my mind. "Yep, nothing to worry about."

"Well, you have a nice evening Ms. Molly," Lucky studied me for a moment, like he was about to ask me a question, then said, "You too Snickers."

I smiled and said, "Good night Deputy."

I left, feeling his gaze as I walked away. I couldn't deny that I liked the feeling.

I was humming when Snickers and I climbed the first-floor stairs to the second landing where my baby blue door awaited.

My cell phone buzzed as I reached for my keys in my backpack. I glanced at the caller ID, I said, "Hi mom. What's up?" into the phone as I opened the door and walked in my apartment.

"Molly, I need you to do me a favor," she said as I walked toward the kitchen. A word to the wise—pour a glass of wine when your mother starts out the call with "I need a favor."

I willed myself to remain open-minded when I replied, "Sure, what can I help with?"

I was starving. I pushed the earbuds into my ears, so I could make dinner handsfree while I chatted with mom.

"It's Granny," my mom whispered.

"If this is about me not taking her to Bingo Night again," I said jokingly, because we both knew Granny Dee hated Bingo.

In my tiny kitchen, I filled a pot with tap water, placed it on the stove, and turned on the gas burner. It was pasta night. I loved Italian food and had picked up a pound of fresh Italian sausage at the village market. I planned to smother it and bowtie pasta with Henrietta's homemade sauce. Henrietta Filadora was Granny Dee's Italian cook and housekeeper, and I loved the sauces and gravy she whipped up.

"Molly, have you been to happy hour? You know she hates bingo."

"No mom, I haven't been drinking. I was kidding. What about Granny can I help you with?" I was in a jolly mood after running into Lucky. Unfortunately, the masked trash digger and his claw-covered paws did a number on his forehead forcing Lucky to leave in such a rush.

"I was thinking of surprising her for Christmas. I'd come in a few days before the Holly
Fest."

This was a shock to me. My mother here for Christmas? Before I could say "bah, humbug!" I needed to know what she wanted. So much for my good mood.

"What about Hank and Carol?" My brother, his wife, and my niece and nephew loved celebrating with my mom every year. They lived in the Dallas metroplex area. And traditionally she'd come to Florida after New Year's.

"He realizes it's your first Christmas there in Bay Isles."

I wondered how I'd manage the Holly Fest with my mom underfoot. "We'd love to have you, but why surprise Granny Dee. You know how she hates surprises." An unannounced visit could only mean trouble at home or Texas.

Snickers nudged my feet. I filled his bowl with food, stirred the pasta water with a dab of butter and salt, and wondered what the real reason behind mom's visit was.

"I think she's not taking her meds and I want to make sure I'm there during this stressful time of year. I could help you out at the Bean Sprout."

The unexpected news of Granny's medicine habits made me concerned, but I only mumbled, "Addicted to the Bean," annoyed by her continued

forgetfulness of my café's name.

"Yes, your coffee bean place."

"It's a coffee house, mom. And why do you think Granny isn't taking her meds?"

"I spoke with Henrietta. She said your grandmother is not eating well and refuses to take all her medicine. Is she using her cane or walker? She needs to exercise."

Henrietta was not only Granny Dee's long-time live-in cook and housekeeper but had recently taken on the role of care-giver.

"Mom, everything is fine here. Granny was at the shop today, and come to think of it, she hasn't used her cane at all that I can remember. But if you're worried about her health, I'll be happy to check in tomorrow and have a chat with Henrietta." Wednesday's officially my day off, but I always end up at the café. At least I'll have time to go by Granny's.

After my morning run on the beach, I could easily pop over to Granny's for a late breakfast. My mouth watered when I thought of Henrietta 's fresh herb, mushroom omelet with béchamel sauce. I knew she always used the leftover béchamel from Tuesdays night's mac and cheese.

"Well, I see. You're managing very well there without my help," mom sighed and sounded disappointed.

I could feel the steam rising from my head like a tea kettle. "Mom, we'd love for you to come. At least let me tell Henrietta so she can get the guest
room ready."

"It's always ready, my dear."

I pictured her rolling her eyes toward the ceiling.

"I guess we could all use a nice surprise." This wouldn't be a surprise to Granny—more like a sneak attack. I hoped she wouldn't be underfoot too much while I put the finishing touches on the Holly Fest and parade. "How would you get here?" The nearest airport from Bay Isles was a few hours north in Tampa, and there was a small private airfield about an hour away.

"I'll call you tomorrow night with the details. I'm so excited to see you and Granny." She did sound excited. It was funny that she called her own mother Granny, too.

"Okay, Mom. I'll talk to you tomorrow. Oh, and one more thing … are you bringing Roco and Bullet?" Roco was her tan, feisty Chinese pug. Bullet was her silver cat with a green eye and a brown eye that scampered about faster than a speeding bullet.

"Of course, dear. I wouldn't put them up in a pet hotel over Christmas. I've already bought their Christmas outfits."

"Great. Let me guess … an elf and …"

"A snowman with a top hat. You know how adorable they look when I dress them up!" she interjected.

Adorable and a bit miserable, I thought. One more reason to let Granny know. She had her own cat, George, and he was not fond of other pets around Granny, especially when they were in costumes. George, named after George Clooney, replaced Elvis, her fourteen-year-old Siamese a few years ago.

"Okay dear. I've gotta run. I look forward to helping you at the Bean and with the Holly Fest. Maybe we can find you a nice date for the party afterward. Talk to you tomorrow. Love you." Click.

"Love you too ..." I trailed off. So much for that. I ended the call, wondering what sort of party she had in mind. Gosh, I missed slamming down a phone receiver. Tapping on a touchscreen just doesn't have the same effect.

I ignored the nagging feeling of apprehension rising in me over my mom's surprise visit and took an extra helping of pasta. With a plate full of the steamy Italian dish, I plopped down on my brown leather couch. I tossed off two blue and white decorative pillows, which Snickers took as a sign to join me. He hopped on the couch and curled up at my side.

I'd positioned my couch so that it looked out the back window. If I stretched my neck just a bit, I could actually see the beach behind the tall palm trees, even though some of their sky duster tops fringed my windows. I loved the palms with their crisscross base and their flowering tops that dropped white buds like snow overhead.

My tiny one-bedroom loft was decorated with chic, seaside appeal. I worked such long hours, that living in a small space never bothered me. Besides, I had a beautiful suite on the third floor of Granny's humongous house. My suite there, where I had lived for several months, was bigger than my whole apartment, and I often still stayed the night after our Sunday dinners together. It was only a few miles away on Oceanside.

My apartment, compared to the mansion suite, had a clean no-nonsense look to it. I was still working on my decorating style, picking up seaside art and collectibles here and there.

In my living room, besides my leather couch, I had two modern chairs (thrift-store bargains) with a painting of the sea above them. My beloved possessions occupied nearly the entire length of the west wall, a bookcase overflowing with my book collection. Besides gardening, collecting books was my favorite hobby, and the book nook in the café was filled with books from my own collection.

The favorite part of my apartment was the loft above my main floor. I had fallen in love with it the minute I stepped inside. The architect had a small winding staircase built in my apartment that led to the turret room. Although the real estate agent had called it the annoying, drafty loft in the end unit, I was enchanted by the cozy room snuggled under the circular peaked roof. It was like I was Rapunzel in the garden tower, albeit a frizzy red-headed one. Who couldn't resist an attic loft with window seats, hideaway corners, towering ceilings, turrets and other quiet nooks?

Fortunately for me, more than half the population in Bay Isles was elderly and couldn't be bothered with stairs to the apartment in the village shops. Let alone deal with another set of winding stairs to the turret room. I had rented it on the spot.

The loft wasn't big enough for a bedroom, but it made a perfect sunroom. It was always brightly lit, filled with sunlight every day. I often fell asleep in the blue chintz overstuffed chair in the turret room reading by a small floor lamp in the corner.

My next-door neighbor, Mrs. Reynolds, was a retired principal and a delightful widow. She was a snowbird and only lived on Bay Isles November through February. She had recently broken her hip, so she would not come to Florida this winter, but would return in the Spring.

When I heard about the accident, I had sent her a care package brimming with my dried herbs. Most of my herbs I grew at Granny Dee's, but I had a few select potted ones in the loft.

After dinner I cleaned up the kitchen, watered my herbs in the loft sunroom, finished five more papier-mâché candy canes for Santa's float, and crashed into bed. The queen-sized bed was in my tiny bedroom on the main floor, where I snuggled with my downy white comforter tucked under my chin. Snickers always chose to start out the night at the foot of my bed on the wood floor, and by morning I often found him curled at my feet on the bed.

An open window in my bedroom that faced the beach brought in a cool breeze. My running top I had laid out for my morning jog rustled on the hook slightly as the breeze passed through. I fell fast asleep.

A soft noise outside made my eyes snap open. I stared at the red glowing numbers on my alarm clock: 12:09.

"Damn," I sighed. I only had five more hours of sleep left before my morning jog.

Another strange squeaky noise from outside made my body go rigid, and my head and wide-opened eyes turned toward the darkened window. None of the noises seemed to have woken Snickers, so I relaxed. It could be a late-night fishing boat in the distance passing through.

"Snicks, you there?" I whispered. His tail tapped the wooden floor three times. I liked to think it was his way of saying; *I am here,* or *I love you.*

"I love you too. Good night."

Two thumps billowed from his wagging tail, as he laid under my bed. *Good Night.*

Before I knew it, I was once again sound asleep.

The next morning, I threw on my running clothes, ate a banana, and made my way to the boardwalk that led to the beach. Through the thick, gray fog I could see my café was still dark.

Through the mist I jogged alongside the sandpipers that walked briskly along the beach, and a lone seagull flew overhead, giving out a plaintive cry.

I turned up the beach and noticed a large log surrounded by seaweed on the edge of the surf.

I jogged toward the log with Snickers at my side.

A horrible thought hit me at the same time I saw it—a body, not a log, blocked my path. A foot in a rubber boot stuck out from the tangle of seaweed. I stepped closer, dread pooling in my stomach. I gawked at the pale face of the grungy fisherman.

I stared down at a motionless figure and my hand went to my mouth. I felt sick when I moved closer and peered down at Jim Grist, lying slumped awkwardly on the beach.

"Hello," I said, hoping he was passed out drunk or sleeping off a nasty hangover. I gently tapped his side with my running shoe. No movement. I bent down and touched his bare wrist. It was cold and clammy.

The Goliath-winning fisherman was dead.

Coffee Solves Everything. ~ Anonymous

CHAPTER FIVE

I fumbled for my cell phone with shaking hands, turned off my music, and punched in 911. As I stared at the man, I realized I was alone with the body. And that's when I screamed at the top of my lungs.

"Ma'am, are you okay? Are you hurt? Please try and keep calm," the dispatcher said.

Calm? I vaguely recall that I shouted a lot of one-word sentences at the dispatcher. "Ambulance. Seaweed. Beach. Drowned. A man, not me. Fell off a boat. I think." I looked around, but even in the fog, I couldn't see a nearby boat. "Come quickly."

"Slow down, ma'am. I need your name and your address."

I gave him my name and the address of my café. "If they park in front, there's a path behind the café and there's a boardwalk that leads to the beach." My voice was shaky like my hands.

"Help is on the way. Are you sure he's dead? Do you know how to preform CPR?"

CPR? I switched from my panic mode to my life-saver mode. It never occurred to me that I could still save him because of the way his unblinking eyes were staring up at me, and it was pretty obvious he was dead and had been that way for a while.

"I'm, um, I'm fairly certain he's been dead awhile." I swiveled my head toward my café and saw there were lights on now. Where was the ambulance?

"Okay, there's no pulse, correct?"

"Correct. And he's very, um …" I felt bile rise in my stomach fairly certain I was about to toss my banana.

"… he's cold and blue." I flashed my cell phone light on his face. "And green."

"Green?"

"Seaweed everywhere."

"Seaweed. Is he in the water?"

"No, close to the water's edge." I noticed that with the tide coming in, each wave that crept onto shore came closer to lapping up on the body.

"Okay, hold tight. There may be a slight problem."

"Problem?"

"The ambulance and help may be delayed."

"What?" I knew the Palma County police officers could be here in less than fifteen minutes.

Calling 911 in our small town works the same as calling 911 in, say, New York City. But there was a tiny difference. When you call 911 in Bay Isles, somebody *always* shows up to see what's wrong. Not so in a big city.

Our 911 dispatchers also work the computer terminals and the National Crime Information Center, the lifeline of law enforcement. These dispatchers know CPR and they know everyone in town and the quickest route to our houses.

"Delayed?" My heart thumped.

"The Bay drawbridge is broken, and it's been stuck in the open position all night," the dispatcher said.

"The Ten Cent Bridge is stuck open?"

"Yes, apparently all night."

The Bay Isles low-level drawbridge was built over fifty years ago to serve the many condominiums, housing communities, businesses, and shops in Bay Isles. The drawbridge was the only link between the barrier island and the mainland. Drivers used to have to pay a toll when it was first opened, and that was why today many referred to it as the Ten Cent bridge.

"There's got to be an off-duty doctor or someone you can call," I stammered.

"I'm working on it." His voice was soothing, much more at ease than I was, but then he was trained to remain calm.

I panicked. If the drawbridge was stuck in the up position, then no one could get on or off the island. No one could travel to the smaller island of Isla del Mar or the mainland and back. *We were trapped.*

Looking back down at the ghastly body, I worried about how Jim Grist had drowned. Did he go out with his friends last night fishing? Where was his boat? Had he been alone?

"Sit." I said to Snickers who was sniffing around the body. I didn't want him to contaminate the area. Why had I thought this might be a crime scene? Surely, it was an accidental drowning.

"Excuse me? I am sitting," the dispatcher's said in my ear bud.

"Sorry," I said, "my dog is here with me."

"Okay. Help will be there soon."

As Snickers and I waited, I noticed the incoming tide crept closer and closer to the body. By the time the police got there, Jim might be floating in the bay.

I flashed my light on the hard sand and saw two bicycle tire tracks bordering the shoreline, and the one closest to the water was barely visible. I often rode my bike on the packed sand myself.

In addition to the bike tracks, I saw footprints and slashes in the sand followed by small holes. I followed this pattern and saw that it trailed up to the boardwalk from the beach. My eyes followed the path to the Village where the Bean Café sat, and my apartment. Could the noise in the middle of the night have been Jim falling from his boat? No, the noise had been a distinctive creaking sound with no water splashes.

The boardwalk ran at a diagonal from the water. If one entered the beach from the café side their footprints would trail from the boardwalk. The entrance here to the beach was too far from shore for the waves to reach and totally erase any marks. However, if someone entered the beach from the Bait Shop side, closer to the water, the waves would eventually wash away any marks.

The tire marks had come from the Bait Shop side where soon the waves would cover the marks and half the steps to the beach.

With the incoming tide, I knew the tracks in the sand would soon be washed away, so I snapped a few photos of the marks with my cell phone.

Another thing bothered me. It was the corpse's position. There was something odd about it. One leg contorted at an impossible angle. I know I once read that drowning victims are almost always face down. Jim's slumped body faced up. And the seaweed looked gathered around the body, versus collected on it.

I rubbed my eyes. I'd only seen one dead body in my life and that was at my great aunt's funeral in a coffin. She looked like she was asleep and was more made up than she had ever looked in her life. The fisherman on the beach looked ghastly.

"Ms. Molly," the dispatcher said, making me jump.

I forgot I held my cell. "Yes, sir. I'm here."

"The bridge is open."

I heard sirens. "Thank goodness."

I flashed my light around the body. Another thing that caught my attention was the fisherman's hands. One hand seemed to be clutching seaweed. His hands were pale, but his fingers and nails were asparagus colored. I don't know what got into me, but I bent down and removed a small piece of the seaweed and stuck it in my pocket. I shivered, thinking that I just committed a vile blasphemy.

Sirens grew louder. I relaxed a little when I heard the sound of tires squealing in the Village parking lot and saw the red flashes reflecting off the shops glass windows.

"Mo!" A shout came from someplace behind me.

"Mo!" he yelled again.

I turned to see Drew "Lucky" Powell.

"Over here, deputy," I said waving frantically.

He sprinted over, knelt in the sand beside the body, and checked for a pulse. He nodded at the first paramedic to arrive right behind him. Two more paramedics scrambled down the beach to assess the body.

Deputy Lucky Drew turned to me. "You found him?"

"We did." I nodded to Snickers. "Out for my morning jog, and there he was."

"Looks like he drowned. Do you know him?" Deputy Drew asked, as he eyed my jogging outfit.

My running shorts were a blinding shade of crossing-guard-vest orange. I wore this color on foggy mornings.

"I believe that's Jim Grist. He's a local fisherman who comes in the café. You saw him yesterday, remember?" I said.

"Oh yes, that's right," Deputy Lucky said, writing something on his pad. "We may need you to come into the precinct sometime this morning for a statement."

"Statement?" *This would be a routine drowning ... or was it? Did they suspect foul play?* "Why?" I asked.

"Because you found the body," he said. "Routine."

Why were my hands trembling and my voice so shaky? I stuck my hands in my pocket and tried to calm my voice. "I read in the paper that he won a fishing contest this past week. It was in the Beach Beacon News."

"Yup, know the guy well," Deputy Lucky said, taking some notes.

A few curls tumbled onto my forehead from my bangs that badly needed a trim. I pushed them out of my eyes and tucked them behind my ears with one quick sweep. As my hand brushed my cheek, my nose twitched, and I fought off the urge to sneeze.

Drew's comment seemed odd. *Had Jim been in trouble with the law in the past?* My mind was racing, and my nose was running. After a few dozen sneezes, and at that exact moment I knew this hadn't been an accident. And if it wasn't an accident, then it was—I could barely say the word—murder. *A homicide here?*

"Were you friends?" I managed to ask between sneezes and sniffles.

"Not exactly." Deputy Lucky nodded to the paramedics still examining the body. The two paramedics backed away from the scene and motioned Drew over while another pair brought over a gurney.

Drew looked my way, then lowered his voice. What he didn't know is that I could read his lips – and everyone else's. When I was younger I had a hearing impairment and was taught to read lips at a young age. Fortunately, surgery had fixed my hearing loss, but my lip-reading skills remained strong over the years.

"It looks like asphyxia," the paramedic said.

"So, he didn't drown?" Drew asked. "If he died by suffocation or strangulation that usually means it was personal."

"I said asphyxia, not suffocation."

"Asphyxia is lack of oxygen. Which is caused by suffocation," Drew said.

"Or when the respiratory muscles are simply paralyzed."

"Paralyzed? How?"

"My best guess, poison. But you'll have to wait for the toxicology test results."

"I'll get with the ME and ask to expedite the tox reports. I'll also get the finger prints and crime scene photos and –."

Drew turned his back to me and I couldn't read his lips anymore.

Poison? I thought.

As the sun peeped over the horizon and the fog began to lift, I distinctly heard what I had just concluded.

Jim was already dead when he washed up on the beach.

After what seemed like hours, which had only been twenty minutes, the body had to be moved back a few feet to avoid the wet sea foam now frothing the beach like a latte.

Several more Palma County officers showed up. Deputy Lucky introduced me to Detective Dawn Lacey, an energetic, forty-something woman with ash blonde hair framing her tanned cheeks. She looked like a model dressed up in a cop's uniform for Halloween. She was gorgeous. I glanced at Lucky to see if he had noticed her drop-dead figure in the tightly fitted uniform.

Deputy Lucky had turned back toward the tarp-covered body and was examining the sand closer to the boardwalk. He was joined by

Detective Lacey's partner, a tall slender built man with a graying beard.

I noticed, the sand in front of the body was now covered in salty sea waves.

The entire Palma County force including the Chief was now on the beach behind my café investigating the body.

Most of the officers, including Lucky, looked perplexed and out of place. These officers broke up fights, helped kids cross the street safely, and located lost pets. Now they had a dead body to deal with just weeks before Christmas.

Detective Lacey fixed on me with a concerning stare, her brown orbs drilling into my green ones.

"Nice to meet you, Molly Brewster," she said, but didn't offer her hand to shake.

"Nice to meet you too," I replied, my itchy nose now settled down.

"Okay Miss Brewster, I have ..."

"Molly or Mo, as most people around here call me," I interjected, although I couldn't see her calling me either. She may have been a knock-out, but standing there she was all cop.

She nodded. I figured she already knew my full name, nicknames, age, birthdate, and any other information she could google on her ride over with her partner.

"Why don't you tell me what you were doing here and how you found the body," she said.

I recited the story of me and Snickers out for our morning jog, and how we saw the body at a distance.

"At first, I just thought a palm frond, or a log had washed up on shore, but when we got closer ..." my soft voice trailed off.

She nodded and made a few notes. "Would you be able to come to the precinct this morning and talk with us?"

"Um, sure," I replied.

"Standard procedure," she added, just like Lucky had said.

Standard procedure for an accidental drowning?

I now knew was not the case. This wasn't an accident, because Jim Grist hadn't been floating in the sea long, if at all. The green seaweed stuck between his nails and fingers, causing the green twinge of coloring on his hands, was not from the sea. It was some type of mint. My nose knew it anywhere.

"What was your relationship to Jim?" the detective asked.

"Me?" I felt my cheeks flushing to match the color of my raspberry hair. "My relationship? None. I mean I only knew him from my coffee shop. Outside of stopping by my café, I didn't know him at all."

This reminded me of the argument I saw between the dead guy and Erica yesterday in the parking lot. I felt my shoulders start to tense up.

"You said to Deputy Powell that the deceased had won a fishing tournament," she said looking at her notes.

I glanced over at Deputy Lucky who was talking to a paramedic.

"I read that in the Beach Beacon paper yesterday evening."

"I see." The detective glanced around. "Can you be at the station around noon?"

"Yes," I followed her gaze. There were a few elderly residents strolling toward them, and amongst the crowd I recognized Aurora. She pushed her way through the gathering gawkers to get to me. Rushing over, she gave me a big hug.

"Oh Mo, thank goodness you're okay."

"Good morning. I'm fine, why wouldn't I be?" I stared into her dark eyes.

"I saw the ambulance and firetruck and the police cars in front of the café. And I know how you like to jog and I thought ..." she stopped talking when she eyed the body, now mostly covered with a tarp.

"Oh no," she said. "Did someone take a fall? What happened? Are they dea ..." Aurora couldn't say the word and held her hand over her mouth.

"Yes, a fisherman is, um, gone." It struck me how no one wanted to say the d-word, as if dead, died, dying was contagious. I was still rattled. Nothing could prepare me from finding a body on the beach behind my shop. And I felt sad, even though I had never really known Jim Grist and didn't even like him.

Detective Lacey's thinly plucked eyebrows went up as she watched us talk.

"Who is it?" Aurora whispered.

"Jim Grist, the fisherman."

Aurora pursed her lips when she heard his name.

"Jim? Was he shot?" Aurora asked.

"No, why would you think that? You're assuming Jim was murdered?" I asked.

"Wasn't he? I mean everyone disliked him. I'm pretty sure some people even hated him. If anyone were to wind up dead, he'd be the most likely candidate," she said.

"He was unpleasant, that's for sure," I agreed.

"Yes, and he was only in his thirties. And healthy. So, a heart attack, which is common here in our community, would seem odd."

"No, you're right. It doesn't look accidental or self-inflicted," I said. "But I'm no expert."

Aurora's comments worried me. Why wasn't she surprised about his death?

"And you're okay?" Aurora whispered. She swept a few windblown strands of her dark hair behind her ear as she focused on taking in the whole beach and body scene.

"I'm still a bit shaken. It'll be fine."

She squeezed my shoulders.

Detective Lacey eyed us. "You need to move
back to the boardwalk," she said. "Unless you know something about the scene here?"

Aurora shook her head.

Detective Lacey's partner called to her. She looked at me and pointedly said, "See you around noon. And please try to keep this quiet," she said to both of Aurora and me.

Quiet, I thought. That would be difficult. Half the island probably already knew, and the other half who were still sleeping would know before they finished their first cup of coffee.

Detective Lacey walked off to meet with the other officers.

"They want you at the police station?" Aurora asked. Her hand reached for mine.

75

"Yes, routine, since I found the body," I explained. I wondered how many corpse-finding-joggers Deputy Lucky had interviewed in the past.

"Oh my," was all Aurora could manage to say, her eyes wide and her face filled with concern.

She knelt down in the sand and retrieved something. "You dropped this." She handed me a pink elastic hair tie. I absentmindedly slipped it around my wrist.

I looked back at the body and saw the local police investigators were up to their ankles in water. The sandy tire marks were history.

You should know that before 10 a.m., no matter what the question is, my answer is always coffee. ~ Anonymous

CHAPTER SIX

Snickers and I were at Granny's house agonizing over the morning. I needed to check out a few items on the home front.

I had stopped by the Bean and asked about Erica. No one had heard from her all morning, which wasn't unusual since she wasn't due to work until the afternoon. I had pulled out her employment application and written down her address in my small red moleskin notebook. She and Fiona, her mother, had the same address. I hadn't realized that she lived at home with her mother. I wanted to talk to her and find out why she and the dearly departed had been in an argument yesterday.

I also wanted to check out Erica's garden.

First, I needed to ask Granny's gardener, Jet a few questions.

Granny Dee's waterside home was almost palatial. I had driven my golf cart over to borrow one of her many cars for the trip to the precinct and took a few seconds to soak in its beauty.

The huge brick and stucco residence boasted five upstairs bedrooms and four bathrooms, while the main floor housed a ballroom-sized parlor for entertaining guests, a large dining room, a library and a massive kitchen, the master and the housekeeper suites and a guest bedroom and bathroom. An attic filled with treasures sat above the upstairs bedrooms, and a dark cavernous basement that Granny called the cellar was situated under the main floor of the house.

The house itself was nestled amongst acres of banyan and jopoka trees, mangroves, and towering pines.

On the west side stood a giant banyan tree filling the space between the winding driveway and the street. When I was younger, and my parents visited my grandparents, I spent hours up in that tree reading.

Stately palm trees, evenly spaced, bordered the driveway, and a large urn shaped fountain sat center before the front porch. The house itself was a beige stucco topped with a dark wood clapboard on the upper floors and wide windows with white shutters.

Even though the house was a mansion of sorts, it always felt like coming home. There wasn't a room that I didn't love, including the fancy dining room we currently sat in.

The smoked apple bacon filled the downstairs with an aroma that was exotic and homey all at once. Granny had just finished breakfast and the three of us were seated at the large table.

I got up and refilled my porcelain cup, and then Henrietta's, with coffee, and then stood over my chair and stared at the herb omelet on my plate. This was my favorite breakfast ... but after my morning, I wasn't hungry.

"Miss Molly, you aren't at your café. Henrietta is supposed to wait on us. Please sit down and let her get your coffee," said Granny frowning.

"I don't mind," I said.

"Hear that, Dee? She doesn't mind," Henrietta said. She winked at me and took a sip of her coffee.

I returned the pot to the burner and plopped down in my chair.

"Nasty stuff, that coffee. It'll put hair on your chest," Granny said.

"A chance I'll take," I mumbled and then pushed food around on my plate.

"Mo, dear, are you okay?" Granny Dee asked. She looked haggard and pale as ash. I thought I should ask her the same question. Maybe my mom was right. I needed to ask Henrietta if Granny was taking all her medication.

"Me? A little shaken." I shrugged. "I guess you heard about the body on the beach." I was still in shock over finding it.

"Bless your heart," Granny drawled. "That must have been so frightening."

My thoughts went back to the scene on the beach that morning. The image of Jim sprawled out on the sand with seaweed curled around his body seemed unbearably sad to me.

"It was terrible. The police want me at the station later." It was only 8:30. I had stopped by my apartment, took a quick shower, before my stop at the Bean.

"What? Why you?" Granny was audacious and fearless, and I supposed she'd rather have found the body than me. Which reminded me to ask Granny about whether she was using her cane.

"Standard procedures. I'm a witness. I found the body."

She nodded. "I don't think it was accidental."

"Why do you think that?"

"He wasn't well liked. I figured someone would knock him off some day."

Under the large mahogany table, George shrieked at Snickers. Granny's cat yowled and raked my ankle. For the next few minutes, the room was filled with shrieks and yaps. I tried to ignore the animals and replied to Granny. "Knock him off?"

"That Jim Grist was a Grinch. He had a history and a lot of enemies."

"Did you know him?" This surprised me.

"Everyone on the island knew him. He hung out at the Grille and I've heard he was mean to all the waitresses."

Mean? I made a mental note to check out the Grille.

"But it was an accidental drowning." Even as I said the words I felt guilty.

Granny rolled her eyes. "Mo dear, please share what you know."

"What do you mean?"

"Eat," said Henrietta shaking her silver teaspoon at me. We call Henrietta our resident foodie. She thinks she knows more about all things culinary than every celebrity on the Food Channel combined. My bets were on her. And I felt bad not eating. I didn't have any appetite, but I didn't like that I was letting Henrietta down. She loved making the McFadden and Brewster households clean their plates. I picked at my omelet.

"What happened this morning?" Granny asked.

"I need to figure out a few things first before I can discuss it."

"But tell me what you know? We're all family here. You don't want your dear, kindly grandmother to be worried," she coaxed, a quizzical half smile on her face.

"There's no reason to worry. I agree with you that his death wasn't accidental, but I really didn't suspect foul play. It wasn't like he had a knife in his back or a gunshot in his chest. There was no sign of violence." But there were signs of activity on the beach. I recalled the thin tire marks and the disturbed sand around the body.

I could have sworn that Granny seemed a bit disappointed that the fisherman hadn't been a victim of a violent crime.

Who would have killed Jim? My own unsettling thoughts were interrupted as I spotted a shadow passing behind the dining room window drapes. I got up, pulled them back and caught a glimpse of a tall figure moving smoothly behind the gate into the garden.

"That's Jet?"

"Yes." Granny said and looked at me and raised her reddish-gray eyebrows.

I knew that look. She wanted answers.

"Can we talk later? I have to be at the police station soon."

Granny seemed to deflate. "You promise to fill me in when you get back?"

I nodded, but had my fingers crossed under the table. How many times had I done that sitting at this very table as a young girl. "Can Snickers stay with you?"

"No problem," Henrietta said, answering for Granny. Henrietta loved my Lab. Granny, not so much.

"Thank you." I still needed to talk to Henrietta about Granny. So much had happened already that I had briefly forgotten about my mom's surprise visit.

I kissed Granny's soft wrinkled cheek, patted Snickers, and made my way to the backyard before borrowing Grandpa's Saab. It was a spotless, dent-free old black car with polished tan leather, and I knew better than to roll down the back windows, or they'd stay stuck in the half-way position.

Her backyard smelt like freshly mowed grass and sea salt, two of my favorite smells. The garden contained umpteen pots and urns brimming with flowering herbs, bushes and ivies. I thought it was the most beautiful place on the island. This backyard was Disney World to a gardener.

I grew up knowing that one day I'd inherit this beautiful acreage and the estate. I took great responsibility to ensure that my grandparents' garden endured and survived. I learned about landscape design and the use of plants. I smiled to myself. I just loved being outside, even in the worst of weather—digging, weeding, planting and pruning. It made me happy thinking about it.

I tugged on a pair of gardening gloves and one of the many reusable cloth masks in the shed to guard against my mint allergy and made my way down the neat path. At one time or another, Granny's herb and extract garden had over eighty plants from alfalfa to wheatgrass. Many of the fall varietals were in full bloom. I passed rosemary, parsley, thyme, tarragon, and went directly to the fresh mint containers. I looked at all the sprightly plants. What always amazed me was the variety of the types of mints. There are more than 500 types of mint plant. Many have similar flavors, and others are quite unique, like licorice, chocolate, grapefruit, pennyroyal, and pineapple.

One thing about mint was that its super invasive. We kept the mint in containers, or they would invade the garden and in time conquer the island. Weeds are like that too. They have mastered every survival skill except learning how to grow in rows.

I knelt down and examined a few mint plants. I delicately removed a plastic baggie from my pocket and compared the few wilted leaves I had found this morning with the plants in the garden. I immediately recognized the mature brownish red stems and attractive serrated leaves with my sample. Even wearing the breathable mask, I instinctively avoided inhaling the fragrance and pollens in the area as I held the baggie next to the potted plant. It was a match. The chocolate herb plant was one of our most popular. *Chocolate Peppermint,* the worn wood stake read. This wasn't just any spice. This was an award-winning perennial that would practically live forever.

The minute I realized the plant on the dead body was not seaweed, but instead was mint, I knew it pointed to someone with a mint garden, or perhaps a chef … unless Jim, the victim, grew the mint himself, which seemed highly unlikely.

Now that I had identified the mint species, I wondered if I should add our gardener Jet, or chef Henrietta, to the suspect list.

I jumped at the sound of a man's deep voice behind me. I whipped around. "You startled me," I said.

He smiled. "Hello, Miss Molly."

"Hi Jet," I stood and gave him a quick hug. His bald head was covered by a Buccaneer cap with a dark ring of sweat around it.

"What are you doing here?" he asked.

"I was, um ... looking for George. Granny's cat."

"George got out?" Jet asked incredulously.

"I think so." *Liar.* George was inside curled under Granny's chair.

I looked around and began calling out George's name. My heart pounded in my chest. Had he seen the plastic baggie?

Jet looked around the garden following my lead. "I haven't seen him today. He never goes far, though."

"Yep, he never goes far," I echoed, quietly.

"Do you need help looking for him?"

I removed my mask and stuck it and the baggie into my pocket.

"No, I'm good."

I needed to find some answers. "Hey, do you know who else grows mint around here?" I asked as I stifled a sneeze.

My questions made me think of my Aunt Tammera, who taught me a thing or two about questioning after years of being married to a detective.

Jet hesitated, avoided my eyes, and brushed dirt off his sleeve. "No."

I discovered that when people fib, they tend to fidget a lot. Jet kept dusting off his clean shirt sleeve.

I smiled and nodded. "Okay. I was just wondering if there were any other sources that the tea rooms buy from."

He brushed the invisible dirt from his sleeve
again. "You're looking at a guy who loves growing mint," He said. "Just look around. Who could compete with this?"

Jet knew most all of the locals connected within the gardening community. So why was he lying about knowing anyone who grew mint?

Did Jet even know Jim? But there I went, jumping to conclusions. After all, it was only a handful of fresh mint. Fresh was the key here. It wasn't sea soaked or wilted from floating in the bay. My overactive imagination came back to earth.

"Do you grow mint at your place too?"

He narrowed his eyes. "Why are you curious about this?"

"It's nothing, really." Or was it? I glanced at my watch. I'd have to work on this later. I sneezed three times and waved my hands in front of my face. "The mint. I need to get out of here. Let's catch up later about the mint."

He looked at me. His gaze filled with curiosity. When had I ever invited us "to catch up?"

He nodded and said, "Bye."

I was driving out of the long driveway when I heard Jet yelling for George.

Coffee doesn't ask silly questions. Coffee understands.
~ Anonymous

CHAPTER SEVEN

The Palma County Sheriff's station was located in a small faded yellow stucco building nestled between Hailey's Cut 'n Curl and Uncle Bob's Bar-B-Q. The lone parking space in front held a sign that read *Chief's Parking Only.*

I parked the Saab on the street and walked toward the police department. My cell chimed in my backpack and I reached for it.

How are you doing? A text from Aurora.

I smiled. My no-nonsense friend always got straight to the point.

At police station, I typed and hit send.

Do you want me to come with you?

THX. No. I'm good. It was a relief to have someone that cared enough about me to be available in case I needed support.

Say hi to Lucky. Smiley face icon. Heart icon.

I replied with a thumbs-up icon.

I was a bit anxious about seeing Deputy Lucky and his team. I wore a chocolate brown short-sleeve shirt and white jeans, having no idea what to wear to a police station to give a statement. My make-up consisted of a dusting of tan blush on my cheeks, hoping to hide my naturally flushed face, mascara, and a swipe of pink lip gloss. I had struggled with my hair this morning, like every morning, and finally chose to wear it down and curly.

Inside the building, to the right was the water department, the building inspector, and tax collector, where residents could purchase dog tags and garage sale permits and renew their driver's license. I had been here several times before to get my new Florida driver's license and Snicker's tags.

There was a small table in the lobby with a sign indicating the entry forms for the Christmas boat parade. The idea seemed festive—watching an interesting array of yachts and boats circling Palma Bay, all decorated and lit up like Christmas trees.

A left turn in the quaint building led to the Sheriff's Department. Drew had once told me the force was comprised of small group of hardworking public servants—one chief, one sergeant, two full-time deputies (Lucky Powell and Ted Walker), two detectives, and one part-time guy who was also the mayor of the next town over.

The receptionist buzzed me through and Deputy Ted met me at the door and ushered me to the interrogation room.

"Would you like coffee? Or water?" Deputy Ted asked.

"Coffee, would be great."

He disappeared for a few minutes then returned clutching a styrofoam cup of coffee.

"Probably not even close to being as good as what you serve in your café," he said as he handed it to me.

"Thank you." I took a sip and scrunched my face.

"Nothing like bitter police-station coffee," Deputy Ted said.

"Anything to shake the cobwebs," I replied.

I was seated on a metal chair in a stereotypical interview room when Detective Lacey came in. *Where was Deputy Lucky?*

Deputy Ted left me and Detective Lacey alone.

Lacey's slender build and sleek hairstyle stood out against the tan uniform. Her shoulders were set firm and she had a strong grip on her pen hovering over the notepad.

She began with my name, address and other formalities and then said, "Tell me everything that happened from the time you left your apartment until the time you called 911."

I recounted how I'd seen the clump of seaweed and how I tapped his boot with my running shoe, how I tried to wake him both verbally and by shaking him. I explained that even though he was pale and eyes open, unblinking, I hoped he was sleeping and I tried to wake him. I stopped and shivered slightly.

I took a sip of my coffee in an attempt to clear the lump in my throat.

"Okay. Tell me Molly, what do you serve in your café?"

I gave a detailed description of my café and how it was more than a coffeehouse. How we served pastries, sandwiches, and ice cream. And that it had a book nook. *What does any of this have to do with anything?* I wondered.

She asked about all of my employees. I told her about them all. When I mentioned Erica, I don't know why I didn't tell her about her argument with the now-dead fisherman. And how upset she was afterward. *I can remember that later,* I reasoned. I wanted to speak to Erica first.

Maybe she caught a look in my eyes, because she asked, "Did Jim ever work at the café? Or with anyone there?" I swallowed hard and realized I had no obligation to reveal anything that I knew or didn't in the case, unless I was certain they were hard facts.

"No, he never worked there. I'm not sure who my employees hang around with."

She nodded but didn't look convinced. Detective Lacey asked a few random questions. "What time passed between when you found him and when you called 911?"

"I don't know. Not even three minutes, maybe."

"How did you know for sure he was dead?

"Um. He wasn't moving. He was blue and cold, and his eyes were staring up." I felt a shiver run through my body. "And I felt for a pulse. There wasn't any."

"How did you know he was blue? It was dark outside, wasn't it?"

"I used my cell flashlight and checked him out."

"Hmm."

A light pink blush warmed my cheeks. What did that mean? What was going on? Suddenly the small room felt like a tiny shoebox.

She glanced at her notebook, and then her vivid brown eyes looked at me. "You didn't try CPR?

The dispatcher said you didn't try to revive him."

"He was gone already." I wiggled in my metal chair, but it and the table were bolted to the floor.

Detective Lacey nodded. She seemed satisfied with my answers. "Thanks for coming in." She flashed me a grin, like she was trying to placate me.

I took the hint and stood up.

Before I turned around, the door opened, and deputies Lucky Powell and Ted Walker entered.

"All finished?" Ted asked.

Detective Dawn Lacey nodded and repeated, "Thank you again for your time, Ms. Brewster. I'll be in touch. In the meantime, here's one of my cards. If you think of anything else at all, please call me."

"I will," I promised.

Deputy Ted turned to Lacey and they talked in a low whisper, while Deputy Lucky walked me out.

"Hi Mo," Deputy Lucky smiled warmly at me.

"Good morning, again," I replied. "Or afternoon. It's been a long day already." I added.

He nodded and smiled. "Do you have time for coffee?"

"Are you asking me out for a cup of coffee?" I laughed and tossed my head back.

"Yes, what's so funny about that?"

"Well, I do happen to own a café."

"True. I was thinking about now, on this side of town."

"Sure. Where did you have in mind?" I tilted my head. *Stop it.* It's only coffee, not a date. But he was so cute.

I'm not addicted to coffee, we're just in a committed relationship. ~ Anonymous

CHAPTER EIGHT

Twenty minutes later over coffee, I decided it was about time to get more information out of Deputy Lucky. Ironically, he was doing the same with me.

I was happy Lucky invited me for coffee after my statement. Apart from unwinding after a bad start to both our days, I welcomed the opportunity to get to know him a little better. He had changed at the station out of his uniform and into a checked shirt, faded jeans and flip flops. I wasn't sure I'd ever seen him without a uniform on. I liked the look.

I had wanted a coffee date with this cute cop for over six months, and now here we were. Even though it was more an inquiry into the body I found on the beach, we did get to know more about each other.

"How does the young lady who sells coffee for a living take her coffee?" Deputy Lucky asked as he removed the lids from both cups of coffee sitting on the creamer bar.

"I like mine with low-fat milk, sweetener and sometimes a touch of cinnamon."

Deputy Lucky carefully stirred sugar in both. "Hmm, I took you more of an exotic coffee drinker."

"Why?"

"Because you're a coffee guru."

I laughed. "I didn't used to be. My parents drank tea growing up, like granny, and I didn't develop a coffee habit until college. And then I would go to the library on campus and drink the world's worst lattes."

"And how did they taste?" He arched his eyebrow.

"Scorched."

We both laughed.

After preparing our coffees, we settled at a table outside in the shade of a green striped umbrella. Even though it was lunchtime, we had bought a plate of scones to split with our coffee.

Before getting to the business of the body on the beach, we talked about our favorite books, mine Agatha Christie mysteries, his noir novels. His favorite movie genre was horror, mine was anything on the Hallmark channel. Even with our differences, we seemed to click.

"So, Deputy Lucky or should I call you Deputy Drew? What did you want to discuss?" I knew he was dying to ask about the dead fisherman. In fact, I was fairly certain this was his first dead body investigation.

"Call me Drew."

"Okay, Deputy-Lucky-call-me-Drew, I know you want to discuss the body I found."

He shrugged.

"What happened to Jim? It wasn't a random or accidental drowning, right?"

Drew stared at me. "Why would you say that?" His tan hid his blush.

I paused. If I was to start a relationship with this guy, I needed to be honest. Was I seriously calling this coffee meet-up "a start of a relationship?" Geez, I sounded like Granny.

"Off the record?"

"You're watching too much TV." He smiled when he spoke, drawing me in with his warmth.

"Well?" I tidied a few fly-away strands of my wild curling hair.

"I'd prefer on the record."

"And I'd prefer to be Martha Stewart. Off the record?"

"Fine." He nodded, then seemed to be about to say something, but instead gave me an appreciative gaze.

I paused again. Oh, what the heck. "The seaweed. The body position. The plants." I blurted out.

"Plants?" He raised his eyebrows. His face flushed, confused.

"You first. Tell me how he died?" I knew it wasn't from drowning, but I wanted to hear it from him. I smiled reassuringly and waited. Man, was he cute.

He sighed and rolled his eyes and let out a deep breath. "Okay. I guess news will travel fast in our small town, so I'm probably not saying anything that won't be gossiped around here soon enough."

"Not from me, it won't." I shook my head. But would I tell Granny? Or Aurora? It didn't keep me from prying for more. "He was already dead, right?" What extent of my own investigation should I share? I wondered if by not divulging everything I knew, was in my best interest.

If he was taken aback by my question, he didn't show it. But curiosity got the better of me. "Well, am I right?" I asked.

He stretched his arms across the table and leaned forward in his seat. At this moment, I became aware of Lucky on a level of being a policeman more than a friend having coffee. "Look Mo, you need to share with me what you know. If I keep what I know from you, I'm doing my job. If you keep what you know from me, that could be construed as obstruction of justice. Now what is it you're trying to tell me?"

"Are you using your badge to badger me into telling you what I suspect?" I said and laughed hoping to break the tension that had built up between us.

He smiled. "I guess, but I like you. In fact, I like you a lot, and we need to work together." He used his thumb to wipe away a little pastry crumb from the corner of his mouth, his eyes full of mischief. At this point in one of his investigations, I'm sure all his female suspects gave in.

"I know he didn't drown in the bay," I said quietly. "And I think you and the paramedics knew that too." I thought I'd take my chances with Drew now versus having to talk to Detective hard-as-nails Lacey again.

He leaned back in his chair. "The fact is, we have an idea about how he died. But you're right, he didn't drown. In fact, he didn't spend more than a few hours in the water, if that.

Paramedics on the scene thought there probably wasn't any water in his lungs because he was already dead, but the autopsy results will confirm that."

"Does that mean it was a homicide, and not an accident?"

We sat at an outside patio table of a quaint coffee shop in Bridgeport. I had suggested the Bridgeport Brews café, so I could check out the competition, and because it was a half-way spot for both of us. Drew lived in Bridgeport, a larger city than Bay Isles, but also located in Palma County. Ironically Bridgeport Brews was across the street from Doughy Delights.

"Pending the autopsy results, it probably does no good to speculate at this point on the cause of death. We're running tests, but what made you suspect he hadn't drown?"

I nodded, more to myself than him. It confirmed that this would be a murder investigation. Why else would his dead body have ended up in the bay.

"You don't act surprised," he said.

I sighed and wondered how much I should tell him? I knew I could trust him. He was a deputy, after all, and it was my duty to follow the rules. But I wasn't ready to tell him everything I knew. Not yet.

"You're treating this like a murder," I said.

Lucky hesitated, as though considering what to tell me. "He was likely poisoned," he finally said.

"Are you sure?" Wouldn't it have taken time to test for that?

"We have ME students, ah, medical examiners," he clarified, "working in the station this week. They ran preliminary tests. We're sure about the poison and he definitely didn't drown. We think he was already dead from some form of cyanide poisoning when he was tossed into the sea."

I was processing what he told me when he asked, "why aren't you surprised?"

"I'm surprised he was poisoned, but not surprised he was already dead. I saw the green plants in his hand." I didn't mention I had a baggie of it in my backpack.

"So?"

"Well it wasn't seaweed."

"You know this, how?"

I shrugged and crossed my arms becoming a little defensive. "I'm a gardener. I grow herbs in my apartment loft and in my grandmother's backyard."

"Well, we're determining the type of plant and then will work to find out where it came from. It's suspicious to us that he had a handful of it."

"But many Bay Isle's residents grow mint," I said.

"I didn't say *mint*." Lucky lowered his cup of coffee.

Oops.

His squinted eyes were on me like a hawk.

"It's not what you think," I gulped.

"Look Molly," he said watching me earnestly, "you need to come clean. Stop hiding information from me."

Now I'm Molly.

I nodded. "On the beach when I checked his pulse, my fingers touched the green seaweed in his hand." Not exactly the truth, but it was close enough.

"And?"

"And, well I touched my hands to my face later," I said trying to remember if I ever told him I was allergic to peppermint.

"You could smell it after it was diluted in the sea?"

"Well, here's the thing. If I tell you what I discovered this morning, will you answer a question for me?"

"We aren't playing games here," he said sternly. "You can't withhold anything." He was

103

staring at me, waiting for my next move. I flipped my hair behind my ear.

"I know. But I don't want to throw out strange accusations unless I'm sure."

"What are you trying to tell me?"

"I knew immediately that the green seaweed was mint. Or, well, my nose knew."

He cocked his head.

"Not by smell. I'm allergic to it. It makes me sneeze."

There was that awesome smile again and it drained the tension away that had built up between us.

"I knew he didn't drown," I continued. "If he had mint on his fingers, and if he had been in the salt water very long, it would have been washed away."

"His face could have been under water and not his hands. People can drown in a few inches of water."

"An expert swimmer and fisherman like Jim?" Someone wanted it to look like he had drowned or had hoped the body would have floated away.

He nodded, and I saw what I thought was a look of admiration in his eyes.

I couldn't help but smile. I was on to something, and I knew I was good at it.

With the familiar Christmas song, *Jingle Bell Rock* playing in the background, I glanced at my watch. I had a few Christmas gifts to pick up before going back to Granny's to get Snickers. I was reluctant to leave, but I couldn't think of a reason to stay longer.

"I have some Christmas shopping to do." I finally said to Lucky, unenthusiastically.

"You don't sound too excited."

"I love the holidays, but the stress level goes up this time of year. My customers seem more in a hurry than usual." *Not to mention there's a murderer in town*, I thought.

"Are you ready for the holidays?"

I shrugged. "Just about. I volunteered to head up the Holly Fest this year, so there's been a lot of meetings and things to do to prepare. How about you? Are you finished with your Christmas list?"

"Me?" He looked sheepishly at me. "My list just got a little longer."

"I get it. Decorate the house. Wrap presents. Solve a murder." I guffawed at my joke. *I hope I made his list. I really liked this guy.* Another thought came to me. "Hey, did I hear that you install tile?"

He smiled. "I do. It's sort of a hobby. I make a few bucks here and there. Why?"

105

"The tiles in the kitchen at my café are loose. I noticed yesterday."

"I can help with that. Does tomorrow afternoon work?"

"Perfect." And it was.

Coffee. Chaos. Wine. Bed. Repeat.
~ Anonymous

CHAPTER NINE

After a quick stop at Doughy Delights to ask Felix a few questions, I ran errands.

While speaking with Felix, he mentioned I should stop and see Jack at his house. I had a few questions regarding the fishing tournament. I recalled how Felix had blushed a lot when I asked him about the free cupcakes. I thought he might have a small crush on me or maybe Erica.

Within fifteen minutes, I was in front of Felix and Jack's house. As I began to walk up to their driveway, I caught sight of the back of a familiar person down the sidewalk.

"Kate?" I yelled. "Is that you?"

Kate Hawkins turned around and walked, practically skipped, up to me.

"Hi Molly," she said. "Nice day isn't it?" If she was surprised to see me, she didn't act it.

"Um, hi," I said, straightening up. I self-consciously reached up and smoothed a few loose curls of my hair. "How are you?" I asked awkwardly, not really knowing what else to say.

"Well," Kate said raising her eyebrows as she shoved her hands into her warm-up jacket pockets, "worried, as you can imagine."

I nodded. "Our first murder that anyone can remember. Bit of a shame." Another awkward thing to say. Why was I nervous? I couldn't control what was escaping my mouth.

"I know, isn't it terrible. I heard that you were there when it happened."

"Nearby," I corrected her. "I didn't see it happen."

"Hmm."

I kept staring at her pink shoes. I needed to shake the feeling that I was self-conscious about finding the body.

"So, what are you doing here?" I asked.

"I was out for a stroll and decided to visit a friend."

"Ah," I said, twitching nervously.

I looked at the number of the brick house we were standing in front of and realized it was the Doughty brothers. "Do you know Felix and Jack?" I asked.

"Of course. We all live in the same town."

"Of course." But I wondered what her connection, if any, was to Felix and Jack since she was standing in front of their house.

"Well, I need to run," She said, looking at her watch. "See you at the café tomorrow."

"Okay, see you then." I stood there a few minutes and watched Kate bounce down the sidewalk, wondering what street she lived on.

After my encounter with Kate, I thought it was probably best not to go to Felix and Jack's house unannounced. I would go later. While I walked away, it dawned on me that Kate didn't ask me why I was at Felix's house.

It was almost dark when I made my way back to Granny Dee's.

I noticed I had a missed call from my mom. *Oh, and then there's that to deal with.* I had been so busy working on theories, about Jim Grist I didn't have time to think of my mom's visit.

Snickers greeted me like I had been gone for weeks. I felt like I had. I needed a good meal, a shower and my bed, and maybe a glass of red wine.

I was just in time for dinner. Henrietta asked me to get Granny and bring her to the dining room.

Granny's bedroom was on the first floor in a separate wing, at the end of a long hallway, about as far as it could be from the living room and still be in the same zip code. The only exit from her bedroom was into her in suite bathroom or the adjoining sunroom.

"Granny, are you there?" No answer.

Had she snuck out through the sunroom? "Dinner can begin as soon as you're ready?"

I knocked again. "Grandmother," I said as I opened the door, peered in and winced at how tidy it was. I had to give Granny Dee credit. Each of the mansion's bedrooms had its own personality, and her master suite was no different. A cast stone fireplace and its mantle filled with photos made the bedroom bright and inviting, and her old-fashioned floral prints in mauve, cream and jade covered the bedding and drapery. A green holly wreath hung above the mantel with mauve ribbon laced through it.

"Grandmother?" My heart pounded. I felt my nose tickle from the faint order of her expensive, heavily-applied fruity perfume.

I stepped further in the room and spotted her sitting in a lounge chair on the sunroom's patio with the TV blaring. No wonder she couldn't hear me.

"There you are," I said loudly. She didn't turn around. Sneaking up behind someone sleeping was never a good idea, but especially a seventy-nine-year-old, some-what grumpy grandma.

"Grandmother, are you alright?" I said as I got closer to her.

She didn't move. When I came around to give her a hug, I saw her blue eyes were glued to the TV.

"There you are. Dinner's …"

"Shhh." Granny pointed at the TV and motioned for me to sit next to her. Her eyes glued to the five o'clock news. And why shouldn't she, since it showed a news reporter standing on the beach behind my apartment.

"Oh no, I bet it's been a circus at the Bean all day."

A tall blonde held a microphone up to her lips and said, "This is Leslie Dallas with breaking news. In the tight-knit community of Bay Isles, a body was discovered today by an early morning jogger."

"Thank goodness, they didn't mention my name," I said.

Granny nodded. "It's just a matter of time, dear."

I watched the news with a worried frown on my face.

A local jogger stumbled upon the body of a fisherman this morning. The Palma County Sheriff' office has said a crime scene has been established near the village, and the northern end of the beach had been roped off by police for a few hours.

Palma Chief police Jameson has said, "We are looking at all options, but at this stage there's nothing to suggest concerns for the community although the death appears suspicious."

Bay Isles doesn't have a forensics unit. However, visiting Medical Examiners to the county have begun an assessment. The police investigation is active and ongoing at this time. We will report more information as it becomes available.

The discovery comes just weeks away from one of the biggest days of the Bay Isles calendar — the Annual Holly Fest.

The annual holiday event and parade dates back to 1931 and is held on the second Saturday every December. It's one of the longest running events in Bay Isles.

The anchor went on to say, "An anonymous source from the Palma County Sheriff's office confirmed that they consider the death of the local fisherman suspicious due in part to evidence found at the scene."

Evidence? What did the detective find? Who was the newscaster's anonymous source?

"Well, well," Granny said. "Looks like we have a murder to investigate. And right before the holidays."

"Granny, leave the investigation to the police." I eyed her. She folded her hands over her lap and looked away from the TV.

"This happened in your backyard, Mo. Aren't you curious? We know he had a lot of enemies, so now which one of them did him in? Things like this don't happen in Bay Isles."

"Times are changing," I said ominously. Boy were they ever.

"Oh, my stars. You and Snickers need to stay here tonight. It will be impossible for you to sleep at your apartment alone."

She had a point. "I should go check on the Bean first. Then I can come back here for the night." I wanted to see if Erica had called the store or anyone had heard from her.

She shook her head. "No, it's dark out. You need to rest, you've had a long day, sweetie. Can't you call the shop instead?"

"I'll take Snickers. I'll be back here in time to watch your favorite show."

She accepted that.

After a delicious dinner of baked chicken with fresh parsley, I took a quick shower and sat on the bed. I logged on to my iPad and searched the internet for uses of cyanide. After reading, I learned it was a substance found in almonds and lima beans in non-lethal amounts, and I wondered if Jim's death was a culinary mistake or a premeditated murder. I know I'd die if I had to eat lima beans.

On further searching, I found another use of cyanide. It was used in photography to develop films.

So, I just needed to find a mint-growing photographer?

Before I shut down my iPad, I searched for wheelbarrow replacement tires to match their tread patterns I spotted in the sand at the beach this morning. I rolled over the image and zoomed in. I noted the features of the tires and their tread that helps make it easy to maneuver and confirmed the load capacity was up to 250 pounds. I frowned when I read that the tire fits most garden and marine carts. *Most?*

I cleared the history on my browser, turned off my iPad, and crawled up the steep steps to the attic.

One of the many wardrobes in the corner of the huge space held castoffs of previous generations. I opened the wooden closet and pulled a red sweater off the rack. With my red hair, bright green eyes, and the red sweater I might be mistaken for a leprechaun. I needed to blend in, so I hung the sweater back up and selected a black shirt with tiny shell-shaped pearl buttons that fell to the floor.

"Why not?" I said.

I opened a nearby chest and shuffled through a pile of hats, scarfs, and wigs. A small wool black classic sailor's cap would work great over my hair. The damp night air near the beach always turned my red hair into wild frizz.

Granny had accumulated a lifetime of vintage clothing and costumes. It looked like an actress had lived here. I glanced around for another item: driving gloves.

I took the golf cart and Snickers, and drove over to my café.

I was in such a zombie-like state, I almost missed my cell vibrating and flashing in my pocket. I pulled over to answer it.

The caller ID lit up.

Well. Well. It was Deputy Lucky, call-me-Drew, on the line.

But first, coffee. ~ words from a T-shirt

CHAPTER TEN

"Hello, this is Molly," I said, thinking that it must have been mental telepathy that he should call, since he had been on my mind all day.

"Mo, this is Drew."

"It is you." I hadn't wanted to come across too excited, and this response said I didn't expect to hear from him.

"Were you expecting someone else?" He sounded disappointed.

"No, what's up?" Why was I reluctantly responding? Could he be calling me to ask me out on a second date? That is, if you could call our coffee meet-up a first date.

He managed to keep his voice neutral and said, "You said I should call you if I had any other questions."

"Oh, is that it?" Why would my brain naturally think he was calling for a date?

"Yes. Did you expect something else? Is this a bad time?"

I didn't reply to that question, and instead said, "I'm headed to my coffee shop. Do you want to meet me there? Um, to ask me questions?" I hoped he'd agree. Coffee twice in one day, that would be my kind of a man.

"No. I'd like to come by tomorrow."

"You're coming to the shop to fix the tile, right? Can you ask me then?" I was as curious as a cat about his questions, and had a few of my own for him after my talk with Felix today.

"Can I stop by your apartment? It's a little more private."

"Depends on what time. I'm staying with my Grandma tonight." He wanted to interview me at my apartment? Alone? Maybe he could come to Granny Dee's. Though I felt quite comfortable with him, knowing Lucky as we all did, and being a law enforcement officer and all, but I didn't want to give him the wrong impression by saying that a meeting at my apartment was okay.

"Oh, good idea to stay with her. I'll call you tomorrow to make sure you're home before I come by, okay?"

"Sure thing. Thanks."

We said our good-byes. I stared at my phone and wondered what he wanted to discuss with me. Did cops make house calls? Or was this social?

Aurora and Bales were closing the café again. They both talked a hundred-miles-an-hour when Snickers and I entered the Bean.

"I told Bales that you found the body." Aurora hugged me. "Are you okay?"

"Yes, it was horrible. I can't stop thinking about it." It really did bother me all day. I was sad over the death, but my curiosity was in overdrive.

"Well, the local News is now saying it's suspicious. If you ask me, you'd be hard pressed to find anyone in this town who liked that guy." Aurora bent down to pet Snickers as he walked by to find his cozy corner in my office.

"You reap what you sow," Bales said.

"Still, that's a horrible way to die." Aurora physically shivered.

"Did the news say how he died?" I asked

"Drowned, right?" Bales handed me a stack of pink message slips.

I had promised Deputy Drew I'd not discuss the death. "It's an open investigation at this point." I didn't look up as I thumbed through the messages. I noticed the reporter, Leslie Dallas, had called. It seemed everyone in Bay Isles had called the café to ask me a question or to see how we were doing. I was missing one message I wanted to see.

"Did Erica call?" I asked.

"No. Not a word from her," Aurora replied.

"That's not like her. I hope everything's okay." I placed the messages in my backpack.

"Nice shirt and hat," Bales said.

"If you're planning on robbing a bank," Aurora commented on my all black outfit.

"Do you think Erica had anything to do with Jim's death?" Aurora asked.

"What?" *Why would she think that? I thought I had been the only one that saw them fight.*

"The police were here asking for her. They said they went to her house and no one was there. Why would they go to her house? They interviewed us here at Bean," she replied.

Bales turned to leave the backroom to check on a customer who had just entered the café.

After Bales was out of earshot I asked, "Aurora, do you think Erica is associated with the dead fisherman?"

"It's just odd that he shows up dead, and then no one can seem to find her. It's like she left town or something. Sounds suspicious to me, that's all."

"Well, let's try to refrain from starting rumors." I tried to fix her with my gaze to reinforce the point.

She didn't meet my eyes. "Is there anything else I should know?" I persisted.

After a moment of awkward silence, Aurora said, "Well, there's another reason I'm worried about Erica. "

I raised an eyebrow. "And that would be?"

Color drained from her face and she nearly blurted out, "She used to be married to Jim."

My brain strained to digest what Aurora had just shared with me. Erica had been married? I stared out the back door. The sun had set hours ago, but it was still tinting the black sky red at the horizon.

"Are you sure?" I turned to look into her dark eyes.

Aurora nodded. She looked worried and a little shaken, and her anxiety was infectious.

"They were married in high school," Aurora said. "No one knew. They went to the courthouse for the paperwork and one of Jim's friends performed the ceremony on a fishing boat."

"But why didn't she ever mention it? And when did they divorce?" I wondered what county they filed in.

Some of the color returned to Aurora's cheeks. "That's the thing. She has never mentioned him at all. Not the marriage thing and definitely not a divorce."

"Who else knows? How'd you find out?"

She shook her head, debating how to answer. "It's a long story. One of those, a-friend-of-a-friend-of-a-friend stories."

"Small towns are always a hotbed of rumors and speculation." My stomach tightened at the inference. It was just too horrible. If they had been married and divorced and now Erica was missing, this would look bad for her. There had to be another explanation. Wouldn't the Palma Sheriff's Department have known it? Detective Lacey asked about all my employees, and not specifically Erica. Hadn't she?

"This could be true. I mean, why make something up like that. Besides, everyone makes mistakes in high school. I mean, you've met the guy. Wouldn't you have divorced him too?" Aurora smiled.

I grinned. "You have a point." My employment application hadn't asked marital status. I could easily research the county records.

My sleuthing tended to be more by the seat of my pants, and I was a go-on-instinct-methodology kinda of a girl but investigating by the book made sense here.

"Did Erica ever work for Jim?"

A slow smile spread across her good-natured freckled face. "Yes, come to think of it, she did at the Island Grille. He bartended one summer, and she was a waitress. Why?"

"It's just that when Felix was here dropping off cupcakes, he mentioned something about Erica still working for her ex."

Aurora paused. "They were so young then. I don't know if Felix would have remembered her working for Jim. Felix used to visit his cousin Jack from New York in the summers. Growing up, the Grille at the Marina had been a favorite hangout of Jim and Erica along with many of their high school chums. They practically had a table by the pool with their name on it."

I nodded. Aurora was referring to the marina pool that bordered the restaurant. Patrons could be served by the restaurant while at the pool.

"Summer time in Bay Isles, especially July, is as mean as an old man with sciatica. We all used to hang out at the pool after a day at the beach or after boating. We used the pool water to get the salt and sand off of us."

Aurora was right about the South Florida summer weather. The endless heat had me visiting the marina pool several times. Last summer was my first summer in Bay Isles and I hadn't expected apocalyptic temperatures, sticky humidity and buckets of rain showers that only occurred during the brief moments of the day when I was forced to step outside. But I couldn't complain about the heat and humidity, that was the price Floridians paid to avoid the cold during the winter months. When I lived in the Northwest, a late snow storm was the worst. By March the only salt and ice I wanted was in my margarita.

"They met at the pool or did they work together first?"

"Hmmm. I can't remember. I do know that after Jim started bartending, he got Erica a job." Aurora shook her head. "We all couldn't see what they had in common. Erica was so sweet and well Jim," she lifted her eyebrows as she met my interested gaze, "he was a miserable, greedy, mean little man." She crossed her jean-clad legs. The beaded fringe at the hem rattled as she swung a foot in irritation, or was she nervous?

"Wait a minute," Aurora said. "Come to think of it, I remember Jack, Felix's cousin had a run in with Jim one summer. It was when Erica and Jim worked together."

"A run in?"

Aurora went on to explain the fight the two had over Erica. "It was more of a scuffle. But insults were thrown, and it was well-known around town the Doughty cousins had it in for Jim."

"Do you think they still held a grudge?"

"That summer they hated each other. Jim was then and still is, −or was −, years later a self-centered, overbearing blowhard if there ever was one." Aurora's demeanor changed, and she had a hostile look in her eyes. "But as far as Felix, well, he lived out of state most of the time, and skipped a few summers coming back to Bay Isles. I never really noticed any conflict between them after he returned. Most people disliked Jim, so it wouldn't stand out."

"I'm going to poke around a few places. Can you help me?"

"You know you can always count on me," Aurora said.

"I need you to look into Felix's background. I need to know who he hangs with, where he went to school, who he dated and whether he has been in trouble in the past and −"

"– why are you starting a Wikipedia page for him?" Aurora gipped.

I rolled my eyes. "He arrives in Bay Isles and then a body appears. We don't know much about him other than the summers he spent here."

I thought about Jim's past. It wouldn't hurt to see who else may have wanted him to be out of the picture. "Would there be anyone else that could have poisoned Jim?"

"The only thing Jim put any energy into was fishing, bartending, harassing people and chasing other women."

I thought about how I had wanted to banish him from the café forever.

"Could there be a jealous spouse or boyfriend out there that discovered Jim's affairs?"

"A jealous lover? That's a solid motive. But I can't see some guy plotting to kill his wife's boyfriend with poison, – maybe with his fists or a gun, but not poison. Plus, most of his affairs were on the down-low."

I kept trying to sort the pieces to the puzzle and kept getting stuck.

"You're right. Poisoning isn't an opportunistic sort of murder. It had to be planned. Someone had to buy the poison and then hide it in something he ate or drank."

"I hate to say it," Aurora paused, "but Erica's looking pretty fishy, if you ask me. No pun intended. I mean there's motive especially if there's any money involved."

I let out an exaggerated sigh. "But no proof. And killing her ex is a little extreme for the prize money," I said, my heart sank in my chest.

"And where has she been? She wouldn't have skipped town?" Her expression softened. "What are we going to do about it, boss?"

I blew out a breath and rose from the chair. "I need to get to Erica. I'll go by her place tomorrow morning." I touched Aurora's arm. "I hate to ask you this, but can you open tomorrow?"

"Sure thing. Be careful. If the police are looking for her, she's probably already a suspect."

I still couldn't grasp that Erica would have had anything to do with Jim's death. But where had she gone? I wished there was something more I could do. Deep down, I was convinced that Erica was innocent.

Then a thought came to me. "Does your dad still have breakfast every Tuesday at the Seahorse with Tony?"

Aurora's dad was the Bay Isles dentist. His long-time friend, Tony, worked in the Ten Cent bridge tender's house. At times, the drawbridge had experienced its share of mechanical breakdowns, and last night was one of them.

"Yes. Why?" Her eyes narrowed.

"The drawbridge was stuck in the up position last night, so no one could go on or off the island. I sure would love to see the video, before and after the bridge broke. Hopefully the camera worked."

"I'll see what I can do. Did you check the webcam website?"

"Good idea. Those are usually still photos, though, and show current conditions. I wondered what it showed last night, if anything."

"I'll ask." Her eyes sparkled with mischief.

"And let's keep their relationship news to ourselves."

She nodded.

I made a quick stop at my apartment before returning to Granny's house.

She was right. My place would have been an eerie place to sleep tonight. I looked out my bayside windows, and all I could envision was a body covered with seaweed.

After collecting a few clothing items and my Holly Fest crafts that Henrietta promised to help with, I left my apartment and walked down the boardwalk toward the place the body had been found. I wanted to check out something.

The fresh air felt great and the combination of sea salt, fishy aromas, and boat fuel filled my nostrils.

When I got to the spot on the beach, I hesitated. A few bundles of flowers were scattered around the boardwalk where the body was found. *Kinda creepy, having this happen right behind our shop.*

A cardboard sign was posted in the sand with a stake: Jim the fisherman, RIP.

I looked up toward my apartment and noticed my window. There was only one other window in the apartment building that could view this spot, and it was from my neighbor's living room. Sure enough, there was a gap in the curtain in Mrs. Reynold's window. Maybe it was my imagination, but I thought I saw a shadow. A minute later, I saw the shadow for sure. I got goosebumps.

The apartment would have been a ringside seat to a view of the body, and anyone who may have put it there. I could stop by Ms. Reynold's place tomorrow. She was gone but it looked like someone was staying there. I figured it couldn't hurt to ask if they'd seen or heard anything.

The noise I had heard the other night still played over in my brain, but I couldn't pinpoint it. It wasn't a boat or car door or any familiar sound. It had been ... oh why couldn't I remember! It had been unique.

"Let's go, Snickers. Granny is going to be worried if we aren't back soon."

He barked at someone walking up the boardwalk.

I held the leash tight. "It's okay," I said to him, but meant it more to comfort my skittish heart.

"What are you doing here?" A female voice asked.

When she got closer, I recognized her. At first. I thought it was Fiona, Erica's mom, but she was too tall. It was Detective Lacey with her hair pulled tight under her hat. I barely recognized her in street clothes. She had on a dark pantsuit and a white blouse, and as she strode toward me her spine was ramrod straight.

"Oh hi, Detective Lacey." I looked for her partner trailing behind and saw no one.

"Well, I asked you a question," she said gruffly.

"I'm walking my dog."

"Out here?"

I tensed when she spoke. "Yes, I live and work here, remember?" Why was she being harsh? Did she think it was a flimsy excuse to come back here? I did have other motives, but I couldn't tell her that.

"I find it hard to believe that you'd be back here at night after what just happened."

Did she glance up toward my apartment? It hadn't occurred to me until that minute that it seemed odd that I saw a shadow in Mrs. Reynolds apartment, and then only moments later Detective Lacey shows up.

"Where's your partner?" My voice sounded shaky even to me.

"He's hanging Christmas lights." Lacey was regarding me strangely. "I'm surprised you're here."

"Well, like I said, I'm walking my dog and …" I tugged on Snickers' leash to emphasize.

"So, you say you were out walking your dog when you found the body," she said with a touch of a sneer.

"This is practically my backyard. I'm here a lot."

"Most people find it pretty scary having a murder in their backyard. And yet here you are creeping through the crime scene."

"I didn't realize this was a crime scene. I mean, there's no police tape and this area isn't cordoned off," I responded. *Did she flinch? Did she reveal something she shouldn't have?* I should be asking her what she's doing here. On second thought, I may be obsessed about clues, but I'm not nuts.

"I'm not saying anything that won't be known soon, but yes, this is a crime scene. Do you know criminals like to come back to the scene of a crime?"

"Are you saying I had anything to do with this?"

"I'm just saying if the black outfit fits, and gloves in 60-degree weather." She pointed at my hands. "If the glove does fit, we mustn't acquit." She chuckled at her O.J. Simpson analogy.

I glanced down at my all-black attire and shuddered at her thoughts. "I like to wear gloves when I drive the golf cart."

Driving a golf cart, that's all I could come up with? I didn't tell her I may be digging through gardens later tonight and I had to wear gloves, or I might be mistaken as a sneezing burglar.

She was smirking, and it didn't look good on her.

"Don't leave the area." She turned and walked back in the direction she had come from.

My head reeled from her accusations. *Was I a suspect? Was Detective Lacey following me?* I stared for a few moments pretending to enjoy the gentle waves.

Why hadn't I brought flowers to lay on the ground? I checked out the tides, noted the time, and left.

When Snickers and I got back to Granny's house, she and Henrietta had already retired to their rooms. I was exhausted.

I promptly made it to the second floor and threw on a t-shirt and flannel dog-printed shorts. I was disappointed I hadn't been able to sneak over to Jim's house to peak at his gardens.

Before falling asleep, I pulled out my red moleskin notebook from my backpack. I had written several names at the top of the page including Erica Alltop, Felix and Jack, Jet M., and the Mayor's son Todd Clawson.

I underlined Erica. What did she and Mr. Grist argue about? I checked my phone for messages. None.

Why hadn't Erica called me back? I'd phoned her several times throughout the day. And in light of what Aurora mentioned, I

132

desperately needed to try and see Erica tomorrow.

I picked up my pen and attacked my list like a maniac. *What could be a motive for murder?*

I wrote down *Ambition.* Would the charter fishing business be that competitive? Under that I wrote *Greed.* Would cheating someone out of the contest be enough to kill someone?

Love. Had Jim and Erica really divorced, and was that what they were arguing over? Had she caught him with another woman?

Money. I started thinking about the fishing contest. The purse was a hundred grand according to Felix. Was that enough to murder someone over? Most tournaments feature modest prize money. Fishing is one of the most popular pastimes in our area, and it could be competitive amongst the professionals.

And I wondered if Jim had a Will. Or Insurance. If so, who was his beneficiary?

What other reasons would someone murder Jim? *Envy or Revenge?*

I read in my Google searches that Jim lived in a neighboring town. I had planned to check out the gardens in his backyard tonight to see if he grew mint and had fallen into his own patch, but it would now have to wait until tomorrow.

My eyelids were heavy. I tucked the notebook in my backpack, turned off the nightstand lamp, and within seconds was fast asleep.

Coffee makes everything possible. ~ Anonymous

CHAPTER ELEVEN

The perfect day started when I could roll out of bed without setting an alarm clock. As the sun crossed the bed in rose and gold stripes through the blinds, I dragged myself from under the crisp cool sheets and light comforter. I pulled on a pair of faded, fraying jeans and a gray long sleeve t-shirt.

I smiled at the Christmas Fairies that Granny had hung from the mirror of the dresser. They had been my favorite decorations growing up. I loved all the whimsical Mark Robert's bendable fairies Granny collected. There was something magical in the winged-elvish figurines. There were three pixies perched on the mirror—a Candy Cane lover, a Choc-a-holic, and the Christmas Shopping fairy.

The doorbell rang. I started down the stairs, only to stop abruptly when I saw Deputy Drew and Detective Lacey in Granny's foyer.

And now my perfect day was getting off to a bad start, as the long arm of the law showed up before I could have my first cup of coffee!

"Good morning," I said, almost choking at my greeting. Deputy Lucky was standing directly under the arched doorway where a mixed bunch of holly and mistletoe hung suspended.

He followed my gaze, smirked, and took a few steps back. "Good morning Mo, um, Molly."

He was so serious this morning, here on official police business. I couldn't help but wonder if my chance meeting with Detective Lacey had anything to do with this early morning visit.

I walked slowly down the wide stairs to greet them. I was pleased to see Lacey looked smaller than I remembered last night, but I still disliked her. Her icy blonde hair was neatly tucked into a tight ponytail, compared to my red loose-curled, I-just-woke-up look.

"We need to talk to you and your grandmother," she said. The crass insensitivity of her demand reinforced my dislike of her.

"What, no good morning, how are you today?" I said.

She eyed me but didn't reply. Henrietta appeared and ushered everyone into the living room. "I'll get Dee," she said, and scurried off.

Detective Lacey eyed the large decorated Christmas tree and garlands on the mantle as she moved to the living room. Her sour expression seemed to allude to whole forests being sacrificed to provide enough evergreens for the garlands and wreaths throughout the inside and outside of this house.

Before long, Granny appeared in the hallway and joined us. She was dressed in black slacks, a white polyester blouse, and a strand of pearls clinging to her neck. It was early for her, and she looked annoyed as heck.

"Well by God," Granny ranted, "this had better be good. I had to race out of bed, put in my dentures and I haven't even had a cup of tea yet." She narrowed her eyes at Lucky, and he blushed.

I was relieved to see Henrietta enter with a tray of coffee cups and a large silver teapot and a plate piled high with pastries and scones, and one blueberry muffin. I wondered if I'd have to wrestle Lucky for the muffin.

Henrietta practically pushed everyone into a seat around the coffee table. She handed each of us a cup of coffee, except for Granny. I was surprised neither Lucky nor Detective Lacey declined. It's truer than you think that cops love coffee. Working at the café, I knew that for a fact.

Lacey picked up her cup and took a sip, watching me closely.

I reached for my mug and stared back at her.

"We need to borrow your cane, Ms. McFadden," she said, still looking at me, not Granny Dee.

"My dear, what do you need my cane for? And which one?"

"You have more than one?" Lacey asked, turning to Granny.

"Of course, I do, dear. I have several to match my outfits."

I thought of all the walkers and canes that often line the wall of the book nook each day. I didn't smile at the thought, though. Instead I asked, "Why do you need her canes?"

"For our investigation," Deputy Drew said.

"What investigation?" Granny asked coyly, as if Drew and Lacey were old friends who had stopped by for tea.

"Ah, the body on the beach," Detective Lacey announced firmly. "It wasn't an accidental drowning."

"Oh my," Granny feigned surprise even though everyone in the room knew it had been no accident.

"But why would you need her cane?" I asked.

"To rule it out," Deputy Drew said.

"As a murder weapon?" Granny asked, trying to fight back a smile. She picked up her cup of hot tea that Henrietta had prepared for her just the way she liked it.

"No. Not that. There were marks in the sand and footprints around the body. We took impressions and well we need to match up ..."

"Wait a minute!" I interrupted. "Are you implying that Granny's a suspect? That's ridiculous!" I was outraged at Detective Lacey's insinuation.

"At this point, were treating this like it's a homicide. And we need to rule out everyone."

"But Granny? Seriously?"

Granny plopped her hands on her hips.

"She has a garden and we found distinct cane markings in the sand at the scene of the crime. So we took impressions of the marks."

Ah. I had recognized the marks. They were holes of some sort that definitely resembled an imprint from the bottom of a cane. The holes in the sand were from the boardwalk side closest to my cafe, whereas the tire marks were from the Bait Shop side. Had Drew seen the tire marks too? Or had they washed away? I'd seen both markings in the sand, but the question was, had the cops seen the tire marks?

"Over half the citizens in Bay Isles use canes," I said, "because most are seniors."

"Then she won't mind lending hers? To rule
her out?" Lacey said.

"How was the man killed?" Granny interrupted Lacey, speaking far more bluntly than I would have.

Great, Granny, I scolded her in my head. *Way to be subtle about getting information.*

Detective Lacey narrowed her eyes. "Well, it's a small town and you're going to find out soon." She took a sip of coffee for dramatics. "He was poisoned."

"Poisoned?" Granny's eyes furrowed.

"Surely you have another reason then for wanting her cane," I said.

Lacey shrugged and looked at Deputy Drew. "Routine."

I was getting more upset by the minute. "Don't you see just a few issues here? One, how would a senior citizen in a small town know where to get poison? How would she know how to use it? And how would she carry the body to the beach while using her cane? And lastly, what's her motive?"

"We're not saying she did it alone." He looked at me with those puppy eyes.

"What? Are you kidding? Me?" I said.

"Mo, you have a few things going against you two."

I crossed my arms in front of me. "Seriously?"

"You found the body," Lacey said.

"We've already been over this," I sputtered.

"Second, both of you grow herbs. Molly in your apartment and Granny in her backyard," Drew said. I felt hurt that he used the information I had provided him yesterday at our lunch. So much for off-the-record.

"Again, probably a third of the Bay Isles residents grow mint."

Lacey jumped in. "We didn't say mint." She crossed her arms on her chest and wore a smug smile on her face.

Oops. I already made that mistake yesterday.

Lucky's puppy eyes were on me again. Granny sighed. Henrietta 's hand went to her mouth and she crossed herself.

I felt goosebumps bloom along my arms. "Look, it's not what you think. I knew it was mint in his hands because I'm allergic to it. It made me sneeze. So that's how I knew."

"You didn't tell us that when we took your statement," Lacey said.

"I ..." *Shoot she had a point. Why had I withheld that information? Again, had Lucky told her?* "... I didn't know for sure. I wanted to verify it, and then I'd let you know. But of course, by then you already knew."

"She told me yesterday," Deputy Drew said.

Lacey nodded. It was then that I realized that he had probably already discussed everything I told him with her.

"Look Molly, you need to be open with us. You can't be doing an investigation behind our backs, and you certainly can't be withholding evidence in a murder investigation."

I nodded. "But I still don't understand why you would target Granny?"

"We need her cane to rule out the markings," Deputy Drew said, while he wrote something in his notebook.

"Okay. Henrietta can you get my canes?" Granny Dee took a deep breath and looked defeated.

142

"Wait, don't you need a search warrant or something?" I protested.

Detective Lacey looked at Deputy Drew, and then he turned to me. "We'd hope you would give them willingly," he said.

"We were trying to spare you the grief," added Detective Lacey. "But I can play it your way, if you like. I could have a search warrant by the end of the day. And a team of investigators that would search this house from top to bottom." Lacey said. "And the garden," she quickly added.

The thought of a team of investigators trampling through Granny's house and gardens freaked me out. What irritated more was the thought that they considered us suspects.

Deputy Drew looked up from his notebook and smiled at me. That always did it.

I nodded to Henrietta. She left to go fetch Granny's canes.

I was angry. But at who? Not at Erica—she had to be innocent. Not at Jim—no one deserved to be poisoned and end up dead on the beach. Not at Deputy Drew—he was just doing his job. Now Detective Lacey, well, she was someone to be ticked off at, even though she was doing her job too, but poorly. I get the whole Good Cop, Bad Cop routine, but Lacey had made me and Granny her targets, with not even a mention of Erica.

I focused on Drew, who was no longer smiling at me. His smile had morphed into a curious grin directed at Granny.

Candles flickered, and holly berries glistened on the mantle. Apple cinnamon smells filled the air, and all was Dickensian jollity, except for the two cops questioning my Granny and me in a murder case.

Life happens. Coffee helps. ~ Anonymous

CHAPTER TWELVE

I watched the Palma County Sheriff's vehicle pulling out of Granny's driveway, smiling at the fact that they had hauled off a bag of eight walking canes. Henrietta had most likely thrown hers into the mix as well.

For the next few hours, I followed up on café matters. Perched on a chair at Granny's desk, I used her computer to place orders to my suppliers and balance the checkbook. When I made the schedule for the next few weeks, I wondered if I should slot Erica in the shifts. I decided against it. Instead I could always pencil her in later. I sent the schedule to my team and reminded them in the email that the Holly Fest was days away.

Could I help solve this murder puzzle before then? If not, it could put a damper on the holiday festivities. Our greeting cards could read,

Happy Holidays from Bay Isles, where the treats are sweet, the people are friendly, and the holidays are murder.

I powered down the PC and scanned the local newspaper, the Beach Beacon. The fisherman's death made front page news. While reading through the paper, I noticed an advertisement for an estate sale in Claus Cove on the same street where Jim's house sat. It was his next-door neighbor's house, the Townsends.

How was I going to find out if Jim grew mint? I needed to check out his garden. If I could get in the backyard of the neighbor's house, I could climb the fence and sneak into the dead fisherman's backyard. After I checked out his garden, I planned to pay a visit to Erica.

I added a few more entries in my moleskin notebook, and then went to have lunch with Granny. I was pleasantly surprised to see Henrietta had set a place setting for herself. I knew she and Granny shared many meals together.

We three shared a quiet lunch in the dining room. Snickers and George danced around under the table, and it would have been a perfect time to tell Granny about my mother's visit. But I had promised not to. Besides, we had a small nightmare on our hands at the moment.

The grilled shrimp panini sandwich with fresh pesto smelled amazing, but Granny picked at her food.

"I'm going out for a few hours. Can I bring you anything?" I asked Granny.

"No honey, I'm good. Where are you off to?" Granny asked.

"I want to check out a few gardens."

She nodded. I'm sure she knew whom I was talking about, without mentioning names. I needed to make sure that Jim hadn't been poisoned at his own house before he was moved to the beach. If he, indeed, had mint plants at his home, and that's where the crime occurred, then checking out the other possible suspects' gardens wouldn't be necessary. But first I needed to rule out his.

"It seems to me that we may have gotten into a bad situation," Granny muttered.

That was an understatement. But would a few cane holes in the sand and the mint plants be enough to make us suspects? What motive did we have?

"Granny, did you know Jim or his family?"

A long silence followed. Granny avoided my eyes and sipped her afternoon tea. When she set the cup down, she patted my hand. "I don't want to worry you, my dear. But yes, I knew his father years ago. He'd lived here before marrying some Chicago socialite."

Panic welled up inside me as my thoughts shifted to the words Granny wasn't telling me. "Were you just acquaintances or …"

"Of course, dear."

"I'm just wondering why the police would think we were involved in some conspiracy to kill Jim."

Granny heard the concern in my voice. "This is dreadful. We'll just have to prove them wrong," she said, reaching out and squeezing my hand.

I nodded. "We have to be careful that we don't implicate each other." I'm sure that's what Detective Lacey was counting on.

"Don't forget to take your garden gloves and mask, dear."

Through the window, sunlight caught the water in tiny sparkles, and a glimmer of buttery hues kissed the mangroves.

I told Granny I'd be borrowing one of Grandad's many cars. I was grateful, as always, that Granny hadn't sold Grandad's collection of cars yet, which allowed me anonymous sleuthing. Even so, if the police were surveilling Jim's house, they wouldn't recognize a car belonging to my grandfather unless they ran the plates.

PEPPERMINT MOCHA MURDER

I borrowed the dark blue Oldsmobile and within the hour, after helping Henrietta clean up the kitchen, I crossed over the drawbridge and traveled to the sleepy village of Claus Cove.

It seemed everywhere I looked this time of year, the water communities did something to celebrate the holidays. But this merry-monikered city really went way out. Miles of garland and holly decorated the lampposts lining the streets. A two-story Santa statue welcomed visitors to the village. Signs around the town advertised horse-drawn carriage rides and boat tours with Santa.

I followed the GPS directions through the Townsend neighborhood and thought about how I could get into Jim's backyard.

As I drove through the streets, I saw neon-colored signs tacked to stop signs advertising the estate sale. I followed one sign to the next.

As luck would have it, when my GPS chimed *You have arrived,* I found myself staring at a small yellow painted house surrounded by cars and a huge florescent sign that read, *One Day Only Estate Sale.* The location was directly next door to Jim's house.

This would be a lot easier than I thought. *I can mosey through the house pretending to shop, but who's pretending? I love garage sales.* Hopefully, the backyard held garage sale items. If not, I could slip out back and make my way to Jim's yard to check for gardens, and if I got caught I could pretend to be lost.

I followed a large group of elderly women up the driveway and porch and into the front door. They were discussing what desserts to bring to Bunco at their church the next night.

As soon as the screen door shut behind us, I noticed a large, bearded man who sat immediately to the right at a table with a cash box.

"Welcome ladies," he bellowed. "If you see a room that is open, then everything in it is for sale. If you have any questions, let me know. Please do not go in the rooms marked, *Do Not Enter.*"

A few ladies asked about porcelain figurines and were advised to check out the kitchen table or ask his wife. She was out back smoking. *Good.* I felt excitement. *This was my lucky day, and the backyard was available.*

As if to read my mind he said, "Don't go out the backdoor. The backyard is off limits, but the garage is open. Maybe you can find a tool or two for sale that your husbands may be interested in. Christmas is around the corner."

One glance down the hall and I could only see two bedrooms. A third door appeared to be a bathroom.

I told the owner I was on the hunt for estate jewelry and old National Geographic magazines. I was directed to a table down the hall. Behind me other customers browsed over the pots and pans in the kitchen and Hummel porcelain figurines on the table. These must have been his wife's collection. Another table held old lamps, ropes, shells and several fishing poles leaned against the wall. A few rusted lobster traps were scattered underneath the table.

I needed a distraction that would enable me to slip out the back door and appear to be lost.

Before I could knock over a stack of the yellow magazines, I saw a pair of shiny dark shoes and tan trousers in the driveway. I inched back down the hall and recognized that familiar saunter coming up the driveway. As the screen door opened to the house, I ducked into the hall bathroom.

Even if the owner saw me slip into the bathroom marked, *Do Not Enter*, he would be too focused on the visit from a Palma County Sheriff's deputy to fuss at a garage-sale shopper using the potty.

Through the cracked bathroom door, I listened to the familiar voice of Deputy Lucky-Call-Me-Drew Powell.

"Sorry to disturb you, but we're looking for a young lady with red, curly hair, around five-five and thirty years old, freckly face. Do you know if you've ever seen her visit your neighbor's house before?"

I felt weak. Deputy Drew was checking on me!

My hair was like a sports car in arrest-me-red. So, I'd gotten used to changing my appearance when snooping was involved. I was now very, very happy to be wearing a brown wig from Granny's attic chest, under a ball cap and sunglasses.

Changing my hair was the easiest thing for me to prepare for a bit of reconnaissance. I always acted and looked older when undercover. After all,
it was obvious that I couldn't just snoop around in
a dead man's backyard dressed as me. I gave a silent *thank you* to my paranoid and eccentric Aunt Tammera, whose lessons were proving invaluable right about now.

As I listened, I pulled my powder compact from my backpack and dapped at my stubborn freckles, concealing them as best I could.

"Hmm," the bearded guardian of the cash box replied. "There's been a lot of people through here today, so my mind is on overload. That poor man next door hardly had guests."

Poor man? He must have felt obligated to speak well of the dead, because you'd be hard pressed to find anyone who liked Jim.

"Let me think," continued the bearded man. "How does she dress? What car does she drive? How old is she?"

"Not sure of her vehicle, but she probably wore a brown t-shirt and possibly jeans," Lucky said.

Ouch, I needed to make a wardrobe change. My coffee-colored shirt was all he could remember? I looked in the mirror and got a reflection of my brown polo, which doubled lately as my café uniform. Okay, maybe I'd taken the *brown-is-the-new black* wardrobe a little too far.

"I can't recall anyone fitting that description. Do you have a photo?"

Oh no! My heart pounded faster. Would Lucky have a photo of me? Would the owner recognize me? I glanced around the bathroom for an exit. A small window about the size of a cereal box was cracked open in the bathtub-shower combination.

"Let me check," Lucky said.

After a few minutes of silence, a lady's voice barked from the kitchen door in the back of the house, "Les, you have a buyer for the riding mower. Can you come talk to him? He wants to know if you have spare spark plugs."

"Okay Gladis, I'll be there in a minute," Les, the owner, yelled back.

"Here, "Lucky said. "This is her Facebook page. Do you recognize her?"

Darn, he found a photo. I was grateful I hadn't updated my Facebook profile page that displayed a younger version of me from college when I had first signed up on the social media site. I looked more mature now and had, um, filled out nicely because I couldn't resist the decadent sweets at the café.

Les was quiet, then said, "Pretty girl. I would have remembered that looker if she had come in today or ever visited my neighbor. Sorry I can't be of any help."

"Okay, can you look more closely. She's known to wear hats, maybe sunglasses?"

I heard a grunt of disapproval from Les.

"Les, are you coming?" the female voice yelled.

"Listen, I can't help you right now. Can you check back later?"

I could picture Drew glowering.

"Can you call me if you see anyone that reminds you of the person I described, or looks like the one in the photo? My cell phone number is on the card."

Thank goodness I had parked the Olds a few blocks away.

I heard the screen door slam, and after a few minutes I heard the police car's engine starting. No one saw me slip out of the bathroom and pick up a floral silk blouse from the $1.00 rack. I buttoned it over my brown t-shirt and grabbed a floppy hat off the hat rack for good measures, plopping it over my hair after I removed the ball cap. I left several dollars on the unmanned cash table for my purchases.

Exploring the backyard was out of the question now, and so was taking the Oldsmobile. I fell into line with the large group of church ladies leaving the property. I walked extremely close to them as they strolled down the driveway and sidewalk, just in case Lucky was still lurking around.

One of the lady's eyes widened as I moved passed them. Even though I wore the floral shirt, straw hat and sunglasses, she knew who I was, alright. She tugged on the sleeve of one of the other ladies.

My heart stopped when they all paused and turned to look at me. *Oh no, now what?*

"We don't want to be rude, but we have to ask," the oldest-looking of the group said.

I hoped she didn't notice my face crumble. "Um, ask what?" I tried to act calm, like the police weren't just there asking about me.

"Did you get that beautiful shirt for a dollar, or were you able to talk Gladis down?"

"Well, you know Gladis," was all I could mutter. "Have a nice day, ladies," I said as I hurried down the sidewalk away from Gladis and Les Townsends' house.

I zipped along over the narrow sidewalks on the adjacent street. I had managed to learn a thing or two about being followed, thanks again to Aunt Tammera, the detective's wife. She would have said, "Molly, follow your instincts, but keep your nose dry." She was discrete too and always "had a guy" who could help locate anybody or anything. I had placed a call to her about Erica and Jim's alleged marriage and divorce.

It had been instinctive when I dressed in disguise before leaving Granny's house. I had a hunch I'd either be followed or be followed up on, not to mention my plans to nose around in backyard gardens. I darted back along a side yard, happy to be incognito, until I came to an alley. Casually squatting down behind a garbage can, I took off the floppy hat and tucked it into my backpack. I adjusted the brown wig and placed my ball cap with the Dolphin patch on my head. I removed the floral shirt and turned it inside out. It would appear white from a distance. I put it on and tied it at my waist, exposing a patch of brown T-shirt. My dollar purchases were paying off. I strapped on my backpack and moved back to the street.

I made my way for a few streets and there was no sign of Lucky or his team anywhere. No unmarked cars followed me. I decided it was safe to return to Jim's street. I had another idea on how to get in his backyard.

But that all changed in an instant.

Coffee is not a matter of life or death. It is much more important than that. ~ Anonymous

CHAPTER THIRTEEN

At the end of the street before Jim's house, I knew for sure I was being followed.

I hurried my walk, and the golf cart behind me accelerated. I paused to pretend to tie one of my black Keds, and got a glance at the purple and gold golf cart trailing me.

I stood up, and a soft, crackling voice behind me said, "Sweetie. Woo hoo."

Woo hoo? I pirouetted to see the golf cart driver motion me toward her. As I got closer, I recognized her as one of the church ladies from the estate sale.

She reminded me of the octogenarian famed for swiping huge amounts of high-priced bling over the years. She looked as tough too.

"Hop in," she demanded.

"Oh, no thank you. I'm on my way to pick up my car. But I appreciate …"

"Get in," she interjected. "I'll drive you."

"Sure. Okay, thanks."

I hopped in the front bench next to her.

"Hi, I'm Corinne, but you can call me Connie."

"Hi, Connie, I'm Mo—um—Molly." First mistake. Aunt Tammera would have said, 'Don't use your real name. Use your middle name or another family member's name, something easy that you won't forget in case you run into the subject again.'

"Good to meet you, Molly. Now where we headed?"

"You really don't have to do this."

"No, I insist. It's getting so darn hot out, and you're wearing a lot of clothes."

I glanced down at my multi-layered outfit and nodded. Maybe this would be a great way to get back to Jim's house. A nosy Deputy Drew Powell wouldn't be looking for two ladies in a golf cart. "My car is on the street that runs parallel to the house with the estate sale. I was checking out the neighborhood and looking at houses for sale. My husband and I were thinking of moving to this neighborhood. Do you like it here?"

She glanced at me for a second and grinned. "Ah, the Townsend house. That's the one having the sale. I'll have you over there in no time."

Connie drove the purple cart as carefully as if it was carrying a cargo of nitroglycerin.

"Do you live here now?" Her voice was crackling. She wore a pink golfing outfit, a pink visor, and white and pink golf shoes.

"What?"

"You said you were looking for homes. Where are you moving from?"

Dang I was rusty on playing undercover. "Across town."

"Uh, huh," she nodded. "Where's your ring?"

"My what?"

"Your ring, sweetie. You said you and your husband were looking to move here. I didn't see a wedding ring," she said as we cruised toward the street near the Townsend house.

I put on a sad face. "Sorry, did I say that? It's just that I've had a tough week, and I was thinking about someone that recently died."

She stopped the cart abruptly.

Oh no. Again, I've said too much.

"Did you know Jim?" Connie gripped her steering wheel.

My investigation could go in either direction at this point. If I admitted to knowing the guy, I could ask more questions. If I denied it, well, I'd be lying.

I adjusted the tight blouse tied at my waist. And coughed. *Geez. I need a lavender bubble bath and warm cup of Joe.*

"I, yes, sort of," I responded, looking surprised, and then sad. I was not used to questions from left field.

"That was terrible. Everyone in the neighborhood is shocked," she purred.

"Did you know him?" I made a strategic decision that today was not a good day to check out his gardens.

She nodded. "We're all just grateful it didn't happen here. I mean, it can be a deal killer on selling our houses. If he'd been knocked off at his house, the values in the neighborhood could tank. A lot of us are retired, and who knows when we will have to sell, or our families on our behalf." Connie accelerated the cart slowly. She was a bit distracted as she waved at a silver-haired woman somewhat on the high side of seventy who sat on her porch. "Hi Agnes," Connie yelled.

"Hello Connie. See you at Bunco?"

"Yes dear."

I managed to keep my head turned away.

We sat in silence for a few moments, until I asked, "You play Bunco here?"

"Yes, every second Tuesday, except this month because of the holidays."

"I love Bunco. I also love to garden. Does anyone here have gardens?" I figured that my conversation could use a little bit of honesty, and I also had nothing to lose.

"Maple and Vernon have a wonderful vegetable garden, but the rabbits are hungry little buggers. They eat half of it. They've tried everything."

"Bone meal?"

"What?"

"Have they tried bone meal? They should sprinkle it in the soil when planting. It makes the leaves taste bitter to the varmints. And they'll go get their meals in someone else's garden." I sank back in the bench.

"Hmm." She scratched her chin. "I'll ask."

"Does anyone grow herbs? They can have great healing powers." I wasn't backing down now off the garden conversation. Plus, we crept along at a snail's pace as she drove about an inch a minute.

"Yes, we have several herb gardens in this neighborhood."

"How about the neighbor who passed? Will his house be for sale? And does he have a garden, or room for one in the backyard?"

She gripped both hands firmly on the steering wheel and turned her head slightly toward me. "No, sweetie. That's a rental house. I believe the landlord already has it rented again. Besides, there's no room in his backyard for a garden. It has a small pool and hot tub."

That was good to know. Google Earth hadn't shown a pool in the photos I reviewed.

"So sad. Was he married? With kids?" My scheming questions kept coming.

"No. None that we know of. He had a girlfriend, or many of them, so I'd heard." Her eyes tinkled. "He liked 'em young and pretty," she added.

The Olds came into view. "Well here we are," I blurted out and pointed at Grandad's Olds before we passed it.

She smiled. "That's your car?"

"Yes, well it used to be my grandfather's."

"My Rudy had one just like it. He loved that car. His was white." Her eyes glittered behind her wire-rimmed glasses.

"Thank you for the ride." I said a quick goodbye and dashed toward the driver's side door, noting that there weren't any police vehicles or unmarked cars on the street.

I watched as she accelerated and sent the golf cart hurtling down the street at breakneck speed, or which to say was about 9 miles per hour.

PAM MOLL

I did a U-turn and drove past the purple cart. I waved at Connie, who now chatted with an elderly man standing at the curb with a cane.

*Coffee, the most important meal of the day. ~
Anonymous*

CHAPTER FOURTEEN

Once I crossed over the Ten-Cent bridge I yanked off the brown wig and placed it and my ball cap with the Dolphin patch into my backpack. The disguise might come in handy later. The trek around the garage sale neighborhood had turned my curly red hair into a fuzz ball under the wig. I removed the inside-out floral shirt which left me wearing my brown T-shirt.

I returned to Bay Isles, starving. Sleuthing made me ravenous.

There would be a free, amazingly delicious late lunch available at Granny's, but I didn't want to have to deal with her yet. Instead, I stopped at Island Grille. I planned to grab a quick bite and ask around about Jim. And I wanted to see if Erica had shown up at her part-time waitress job.

The Island Grille was a quaint standalone building, painted turquoise and white with a huge Marlin mounted above the front door. It was the last building situated in the town's marina. It was a popular spot for fishermen, and I had heard that Jim ate there often.

The patio table I chose sat out back with views of the Grand Canal. There were only a few other patrons in the restaurant enjoying a late lunch al fresco. A large chalkboard showed the catch of the day and other specials.

Within a few minutes, a tiny blonde-haired, blue-eyed waitress with a ponytail approached the table. "Hi, I'm Amy. You're the coffee shop lady, right?"   She chewed and snapped her gum, bobbing her head like a pigeon with an attitude.

"Yes, hi. I'm Molly." I smiled.

"Nice to make your acquaintance. I've seen you at the Bean a few times, and my bestie told me she works for you part-time."

"Erica?"

"Yes. Can I bring you something to drink?"

"Sweet tea."

"Do you know yet what you're having to eat? The house salad with grilled shrimp is great. Not that you need it. If I had your body, I wouldn't be covering it up in a baggie t-shirt."

"Um, thanks," I said. "Shrimp salad it is."

"I'll get the kitchen started on the salad. By the way I love your hair," Amy gushed. "I've been thinking about dyeing my own hair a fun color."

"I think blonde is the perfect color for you."

"Thanks," Amy gave me a nod and scurried off.

I was thrilled at my luck to be sitting at the table waitressed by none other than Erica's bestie! I tried to contain my obvious excitement.

Amy returned with a tall glass of iced tea with a lemon wedge.

"Thanks," I said, squeezing the lemon into the tea. "Your friend Erica is amazing. Did you know her mom works at the Bean part time too?" I wanted to strike up a conversation and ask questions without sounding like a detective. I took a sip of the tea.

"I did know Fiona worked there too. They both make killer lattes. Did you know, they own an espresso machine?"

I nodded, as if I knew about their kitchen appliances. I did know they lived together. What else should I have known about Erica?

"Isn't it just crazy what happened to Jim?" I stirred my tea.

Amy's blue eyes betrayed a sort of smoldering bitterness I wouldn't have thought possible in this lovely young waitress with a wide smile.

"That worm was always in here picking on Erica. Her first day on the job, he didn't waste any time trying to get to her."

"Did they date?"

"That whack job. He flirted with everyone and anybody. I heard he used to work here years ago." She shrugged. "No matter. He's gone and I'm not sorry about that." Her expression darkened even more. A blush filled her cheeks.

"That swine took advantage of my good friend," she whispered angrily. "Jim's death couldn't have happened to a more deserving man."

I started to ask her another question, but stopped when an elderly couple walked in, and caught Amy's eye. They sat a few tables from me.

Amy waved at the couple. "Be with you all
in a minute. Coffee?"

The woman with yellowed gray hair pulled tightly back from her weathered face into a ponytail yelled back to Amy. "Bob likes his black."

Amy nodded.

Before I lost Amy to the couple, I wanted to find out more about Jim and Erica's relationship.

"What reasons could you think that someone would want him knocked off?" I said very reasonably, without emotion.

The blonde waitress counted them off on her fingers. "Scumbag. Deadbeat. Cheat. Liar. Fraud."

She smiled and went in search of two cups of coffee. Before she was out of earshot, she turned back to me and said loudly, "Oh, and he never tipped, so add cheapskate to that list."

Sorry I asked.

I finished my salad, not leaving even a shred of lettuce or crouton on the plate. Amy had been right—it was amazing! I couldn't get over how many restaurants served shrimp and seafood. Even with my rabbit diet and fresh seafood, I had gained weight since moving to Bay Isles. My mom was always worried about it, while Granny said I looked *healthy*. It felt good to put on a few extra pounds. My ex-boyfriend had been a little too worried about waistlines and appearances. I guess that's one of the many reasons he was my ex.

Amy brought me the check and lingered at my table long enough for me to ask a few more questions.

When the conversation got back to Erica and Jim, I said, "I'm curious about their relationship. Were they close?"

When Amy hesitated, I added, "I know they were an item."

She nodded. "I'm glad it's over. He owes her money, and that's why she lives with her mom. It's crazy. She has to work two jobs, live at home, and he wins a big prize at the fishing tournament. And he won't share a dime of it. Such a loser."

I grimaced. *Had Erica tried to get money from Jim? Would that be enough of a motive?* My mouth was dry.

"Have you seen Erica lately? Do you know where she's at? Did she see him, I mean, before he died?" *Where was Erica now? Why hadn't she showed up for work? And where was she the night of the murder?*

Amy shook her head. "She's been sick, or she says she is. I think she's hiding from the press. Me, I'd be out celebrating."

Why hadn't Erica called in when she missed her shift? I would have understood why she didn't want to work.

170

"The news people are saying he was dead before he was dumped in the water." Amy's icy blue eyes stared at me.

I nodded. "I heard that." It was true. The latest news mentioned the police were now calling the fisherman's death a homicide.

Amy tugged on her ponytail and tilted her head. "Hey, you don't think they would suspect Erica in any wrongdoings?"

"At this point, I'm sure they're considering everyone that knew him a suspect."

"Wow. I need to call her after my shift. We need a serious girl's night out." She looked worried.

"Do you know others he dated? Or anyone else that may have wanted him ...," I stopped, and chose my words carefully, "...um, wanted him out of the way?"

She thought hard. "Like I said, you'd be hard pressed to find anyone who did like him." She grinned. "But there was this one lady he had a drink with. I wasn't here, but Missy saw them together. I remember, because she told me about it the next
day."

"Missy?"

"The bartender."

"Did Missy describe her to you?"

"All I remember is she had called her *an older lady*."

"Older? As in his mother type old? Or his grandmother?"

"No, not that. Just she didn't look his age. Jim always preyed on younger women. She just wasn't his normal type."

"I see. Is Missy working today?" I'd like to talk to her.

"No, she doesn't work lunch. She might work later tonight. She'll be bartending at the Tiki bar for sure on Friday night." Amy gestured toward the thatched roof structure closer to the water.

I nodded. The Island Grille's Tiki Bar sat at the end of the patio with views of all the boats moored at the marina. The boats ranged from sixty-foot yachts to a small dinghy that looked pretty much like a bathtub with an outboard motor attached to it. The Tiki Bar was recently added to accommodate the overflow on weekends when the restaurant's tables were full. It was a boisterous watering hole, and locals bellied up to it every night.

I paid my check, leaving Amy an extra-large tip. I was digging in my backpack when I heard footsteps come up to the table.

"Hello Mo."

I looked up and found Deputy Lucky's compelling blue eyes staring at me. He was in uniform; his face was flushed, and he looked alarmingly handsome.

"Hello," I said, sounding foolishly nervous. "Are you following me?"

He grinned. "No. I thought I'd come here to ask around about Jim." His smile vanished, and he cocked his head as if a thought just occurred to him. "Hey, you aren't doing the same, are you? You wouldn't be interfering in a police investigation, would you?"

A wave of guilt washed over me. I had been so focused on proving my innocence and trying to find the murderer, I'd never stopped to think of what it might seem like from Drew's standpoint.

"I'm just here eating lunch," I finally managed, but couldn't look him in the eyes.

"Un, huh," he said eyeing me suspiciously.

Amy returned for the check and cash. She eyed Drew when she picked up the money. "Thank you," Amy said.

I exhaled when she turned to walk away without even a word to me about our previous conversation. Then she stopped, turned and said, "I confirmed that Missy works tonight and tomorrow night if you want to stop by and talk to her about– "

"– thank you. I will ask her about that drink recipe," I said, cutting her off. Amy shrugged and walked away.

Lucky narrowed his eyes at me and I saw the shift in his expression from Lucky the man whom I hoped would ask me out to dinner to Deputy Lucky that suspected me meddling in his case.

"Mo, I realize that you're asking questions around town and you only mean to help your friends, but I need to remind you to leave the detective work to law enforcement."

"Of course," I said, praying I sounded convincing.

"Okay then. Have a nice day," Drew said eyeing me.

"You too, deputy." I twisted my hair nervously.

He turned and before taking one step, he turned back around. He leaned forward and lowered his voice. "One question, why would you need a drink recipe from a bartender? You're not thinking of serving alcoholic coffee drinks at your café, are you? Because that's a crime in this state. "

"Like the leash laws?"

He blushed.

"The drink recipe is for Granny's party," I said, as I struggled to maintain a blank expression. "Last I checked it was still legal to serve alcohol in your home."

He gave me an amused smile. "Is that the best you can do?"

"I have no idea what you're talking about."

"You wouldn't be hanging out with the bartender to find out who the deceased patronized with?"

Crap! I shook my head.

He winked and then sauntered off to the busboy station to talk to a couple of waiters.

Before stopping by Granny's house, I sat in the Olds and retrieved my red moleskin notebook from my backpack. I wrote on my list, *Mystery date*, and then underneath it added, *Talk to Missy tomorrow.*

I circled Erica's name at the top of my list. Next to it I had written: *motive and a question mark.* I crossed out the question mark and wrote: *money, divorce.*

My heart sank. I just knew that it wasn't Erica. I had so many questions for her. Even as I drove back to Granny's house, I tried to convince myself that Erica had nothing to do with the death.

But I had a problem with the theory. Several problems, actually.

I desperately wanted to talk to Erica, but she wasn't returning my texts or calls. And she didn't show up for work. Normally that could be an employment-ending move, but I felt there had to be a reason behind it.

I managed to swing by Granny's house and sneak in while she and Henrietta were in their rooms. I changed into a pair of jogging shorts, running shoes, and a tank top. I grabbed Snickers' leash.

"Come on, boy," I whispered. "Let's go for a walk." I had deposited the Olds in the garage, and in turn grabbed the golf cart. The plan would be to get close to Erica's house, leave the cart, and walk Snickers to nonchalantly "stumble" on her residence. From there, well, I would have to wing it.

Like all my employees, Erica and her mom lived in the patchwork of our tiny community. I

176

drove slowly down the crisscrossed streets that on a map resembled a fishtail's bones with each splinter leading to water. The houses on the main spine of the tail didn't have water access. However, many of the homes were situated on canals and had boat access.

The sun was hiding behind dark clouds, making it appear dusk outside. While I looked for a place to park the cart, I thought of Deputy Drew.

What would he think of me investigating the murder? It hadn't been 48 hours, and I managed to hide from Drew in disguise, possibly commit two potential misdemeanor crimes, sicced a raccoon on him, and stumbled upon a murder scene. For the first time since I left Oregon, I felt I might never be a potential date for the handsome Deputy Lucky Drew Powell.

I parked the golf cart a few blocks from Erica's street, and Snickers and I walked toward 4th Avenue. When I got to her house, I noticed there were several lights on. *Good, someone was home.*

House number seven was a one-story bungalow in the cul-de-sac. Two-foot-high plastic candy canes lined the sidewalk leading to the front door. A deflated Santa and reindeer lay in heaps on the grassy lawn. The gardens were colorful and perfect. With the manicured landscape and trimmed bushes, I wondered if this attention to detail meant that Erica or her mom had a garden out back. A garden with mint? Chocolate Peppermint?

I tried to recall if Erica had ever expressed an interest in the fresh herbs at the café. But she never had. I hated to think Erica would be a suspect in the fisherman's death, but if Aunt Tammera found out that Erica and Jim were married, then there could be a motive. What could have gotten into her? Jealousy? Money? Divorces can be nasty, but murder?

I shivered.

Snickers and I walked up the neatly trimmed path to her house. I rang the doorbell but couldn't hear the chimes inside the house. I waited a few minutes and rang it again.

"Maybe her doorbell is broken," I said to Snickers. I knocked on the red painted door, and then looked at Snickers. "Or maybe she's in the shower or stepped out."

When she still hadn't answered. I rapped a little harder and the door gave a little. It creaked open.

Startled that Erica would leave her door open, I stuck my head in and yelled out, "Erica, it's Molly." I pushed the door completely open and stepped in.

"Stay," I said to Snickers. He obediently sat on the rubber welcome mat.

The minute I stepped into the foyer, I could smell coffee brewing and Erica's perfume.

"Hello Erica," I yelled. "Your front door was open."

I walked into the foyer and hesitated. I felt a pang of homesickness when I noticed some of the Christmas decorations were similar to the ones my mom had used while growing up in the Northeast. A carved wooden nativity scene and delicate pastel angel figurines lined an antique Bombay chest, and a large Santa sat next to it.

"Hello," I said again. "I tried calling you."

Suddenly I heard a crash coming from what must be the kitchen. I turned left toward the noise and I heard movement, followed by silence.

"Erica, it's Molly. Snickers and I were out walking, and I wanted to drop in to see how you're feeling."

There wasn't a response. So, I took a few steps toward the kitchen. I screamed out when a grey Siamese cat darted in front of me. I whirled around, my eyes following the cat. Snickers nudged his nose through the front door, leaped in the foyer, and chased and barked at the cat.

"Stop, both of you." I scolded at him and

Erica's cat. Both immediately calmed down and the eerie silence filled the house again. I was concerned when Erica hadn't come out after hearing all the ruckus.

"Erica, are you okay?"

I walked into the kitchen, and she wasn't there. I smiled when I noticed a shiny espresso maker on the counter. Since owning the Bean, the hissing and sputtering of the espresso machines were music to my ears.

A decorated tree, at least 8-foot high, filled a corner of the family room situated off the kitchen. I turned toward the tree and felt relief when I saw Erica sleeping. I could see her legs hanging loosely off the side of the couch from the back. Not wanting to startle her awake, I said loudly, "Hi, it's me Molly."

The complete silence and the strong odor of over-brewed coffee sent a little flutter in my gut. As I stepped around to the front of the couch, I screamed at the top of my lungs.

Erica's fair skin was pale white and there was blood dripping down her face. Her auburn hair a tangled mess and her eyes closed.

Get a grip, I said to myself. *Erica needs help.*

"Erica, oh my. Wake up." *Please don't be dead. Please.*

I knelt down on the thick carpet in front of the couch and took Erica's wrist. There was a pulse, thank God.

Get help, my shocked mind told me. *Get help!*

You can do hard things. Love, Coffee. ~ Anonymous

CHAPTER FIFTEEN

I pulled out my cell phone, and with shaky hands I dialed 911. The operator was calm as I yelled fragmented sentences into the phone. "My employee, ah, my friend, she's been hurt. She fell and hit her head." As I said the words, I wondered how could Erica have fallen so perfectly on the couch with that gash? And then there was the matter of the front door left opened. "Please send help. She's unconscious, but she's breathing. Hurry, please!"

"Ma'am," The operator intoned. "Keep calm."

Right. Keep calm, Mo, think of Erica. I tried to prop a pillow under her head and felt sticky, matted hair. I realized it was blood and heard myself screaming again.

"Hello," came a disembodied voice from my cell. "Hello ma'am. Are you okay?" the operator asked in a level voice.

I calmed down again and managed to say, "Sorry I'm just rattled. Blood. There's a lot of it."

"I'll dispatch paramedics to you, but first I'll need your location."

"4th street." I yelled into the phone. "Um." I had forgotten Erica's house number. "The last house in the cul de sac. The red door. It's open."

"Okay, sending help now."

I reach for Erica's hand and held it. It felt warm. My heart was pounding. "Hang in there, girl. Help is on the way." I tried to soothe her as I rubbed her pale hand. I reached for a blue and baby pink crocheted afghan on the overstuffed chair and covered her with it.

I could barely hear the dispatcher's voice. "Sorry?" I said.

"What's your friend's name?" He repeated.

"Sorry, yes, her name is Erica Alltop." I stared at the spots of blood that had transferred to my hand when I touched her head wound.

"And your name?" The dispatcher was doing his job. I just wanted help to arrive before it was too late.

"I'm Molly. Molly Brewster. I stopped by to see how she was feeling because she's missed work for a few days, and I found her unconscious." Why was I explaining myself to the 911 operator? Was I subconsciously worried about how this would look? Two bodies in one week? As Aunt Tammera would have said, "Run Mo, run."

"Okay Molly. Do you have something to press to her head to help stop the bleeding?"

"No, but I can find something."

I placed my mobile phone on speaker and with trembling legs rushed into the kitchen. I saw Snickers laying under the table and the Siamese cat on top of it. I was pretty sure Erica didn't allow her cat on the kitchen table, but at this point I wasn't going to shoo it down. The cat must have approved of my decision, because it flicked its long furry tail.

There were several towels draped over the chrome handles of both the dishwasher and the oven doors. I didn't want to chance that they were soiled, so I opened a few drawers. Jackpot. I grabbed a handful of brightly colored towels and rags.

"I have a clean dishtowel," I said into my phone as I stood over Erica's auburn, totally unconscious head. I closed my eyes for a few seconds and took a deep breath. *I can do this.*

"Okay, Molly, can you see the wound?"

"I'm not sure. There's so much blood on the couch and her hair."

184

"Gently press it to the wound. Be careful of her neck."

My hands were shaking, and I was fighting
back tears, but I did as he said.

"Erica," I said gently. "Stay with us. Hang on."

While waiting for help to arrive, it's moments like this that I wished I lived in a larger city. A city with its own police force, and CSI, and a hospital. Even though Bay Isles shared these facilities with neighboring cities, there was still lag time.

I heard Snickers whimper and the cat let out a loud meow.

"Shhh," I said to Snickers and Erica's cat.

"Did you shush me?" The dispatcher asked.

"Sorry, no I meant the animals."

Within a few minutes, I heard sirens out front and soon saw a familiar person rush into the room.

Deputy Drew looked at me, perplexity written on his face. "Mo?" he said. *Again?* Well, he didn't say that part, but it was written on his face.

"Hi," I forced a sweetish smile between clenched teeth.

Deputy Drew's face recoiled when he saw Erica. "Is she …" Deputy Drew shot a look at me, then back at Erica.

"There's a pulse."

He nodded. "Good. Help is on the way." He frowned. "What are you doing here?" He leaned down to inspect Erica.

My mind groped for a reasonable explanation for my appearance in Erica's living room, holding her hand. The truth was always the best policy. Unless you were Aunt Tammera. She could weave fiction out of facts and have you believing they were true.

"This is just awful. I came to check on her. She wasn't returning my calls or texts. She hadn't shown up for work yesterday, and no one could get a hold of her."

How could he look at me that way? Surely, he didn't think I had anything to do with Erica's injury?

I cocked my head to the side when I heard his wonderful soothing voice. I shook my head to clear it and wondered what he had wanted when he said he needed to stop by my apartment to chat.

"I'm sorry, what did you say?" I felt a blush climb my cheeks as I thought about how I'd been staring at him. But anything was better than thinking of Erica lying on the couch. I shuddered.

"What happened to her?" Lucky rubbed his forehead.

"I can see how this looks."

"How does it look?" He raised his eyebrows.

"I mean I found a body on the beach, and now I find Erica hurt."

His faced flushed. "Okay, so can you tell me what happened to her?"

"No. I mean I have no idea what happened to Erica. I wanted to check on her."

"Check on her? Why?"

"Um," I was willing to tell him everything this time. "I remembered that she had words outside the café with Jim." I felt guilty telling him this about Erica, when I hadn't been able to talk to her first.

"Jim Grist?"

I nodded.

"What about?"

"I don't know. And then I got worried when she hadn't shown up for work."

"So, is it common for a boss to check on her employees?"

"No, I supposed not. But I was worried about her. And, I ..."

He didn't reply. He blinked. "And you, what?"

"What?" I said.

"You said you were worried about her and, then what?"

"The door was open."

"Unlocked and open?"

"Yes."

"Didn't that seem a bit bizarre?"

"What?" I sputtered.

"The door being left open."

"No, I mean we are in a small town and many of the residents leave their doors unlocked."

"And you know this how?"

He was getting to be annoying. I was confused and shaky still from finding Erica with blood all over the back of her head. "Don't you need to go secure the place or something?" I looked around.

"Yes. Help is on the way. I wanted to ask you some questions first before I have a look around."

"It's just that I'm a bit shaken up still."

"I can imagine. First you find a body right outside your apartment. And not even a day later you come across one of your employees injured, and possibly it's an attempted murder."

"Oh geez." My fingers felt cold against my cheeks. This doesn't look good for me. I needed to find out the person behind these two acts before the police suspected me.

I heard the sirens and the ambulance arrived within minutes, its flashing lights illuminating the driveway. Two paramedics rushed into the family room, rolling a stretcher between them.

"You'll need to step aside, ma'am," one of them told me. I realized I was still holding Erica's hand. I nodded and moved aside. Tears welled up in my eyes.

Deputy Drew led me out of the way, so the paramedics could work on Erica. One talked on the radio and took instructions.

"Looks like a serious head injury," The younger paramedic said to Deputy Drew.

"Is she going to be alright?" I asked, brushing away a tear.

"We don't know yet. We'll get her to the hospital and they'll find out what kind of shape she's in."

They secured her neck in a brace and slid a backboard under her and bandaged her head.

Lucky guided me to the kitchen. From there I heard the EMT's speaking in low, urgent voices.

"Should I go to the hospital?" I asked Lucky.

"You can follow in your car. Oh wait, where's your car?" He asked, puzzled.

"We were out walking …" I said, pointing at Snickers. I decided not to tell him about the golf cart two streets over.

"I can take you in my car, if you like."

"I'll need to call Erica's mom, Fiona. She's on a cruise, so I'm not sure her cell will work. But I can contact the ship."

"You might want to go home and clean up first." Drew used a corner of a white towel to wipe something from my face. When I saw that it was blood, I felt the room spin.

"Are you okay?" he said, grabbing my arm.

I nodded. "I guess." I sighed weakly.

His hands touched my jaw briefly, igniting a spark in me. Then he glanced at the paramedics and his face transformed back to business. "We'll need you to come to the station, again. To take your statement."

"Take my statement? Why?"

"Because you found her."

"Uh, okay." That sounded reasonable. But I didn't like the idea of having to go to the police station to discuss Erica.

Detective Lacey, the woman with the granite face, walked into the kitchen. She strode toward us like a matador, and I'm surprised that no one else could hear the sarcastic click of her heels as they hit the well-polished tile floors. She was as frigid as an iceberg.

Lucky took a giant step and slid between me and Detective Lacey. He said a few words so low, I couldn't hear them. I was hoping they'd turn in my direction, so I could read their lips.

While the paramedics worked on Erica, Detective Lacey came over to me. "Miss Brewster, seems we keep meeting."

I nodded and sighed.

"Tell me what happened here?"

For a few minutes, I went over how I'd found Erica. I answered her questions, just like I had with Deputy Drew.

"Do you think she let in whoever did this?" I asked.

"I'll ask the questions. You came here to talk to her, right?"

"I hadn't actually talked to her. She was not at work. Snickers and I were out walking, and I wanted to check on her."

"Isn't that quite a walk from your apartment?"

"I'm staying at Granny's and …"

"Right. And how long were you here?"

"Like I told Drew, um, Deputy Drew, I was at the Grille eating a late lunch. You can ask Amy the waitress." I almost added that she should ask Drew, because he saw me too, but I'd let him tell Lacey that.

Detective Lacey nodded to Drew.

Deputy Drew left the room, telling me he'd be right back.

A few minutes later, he returned. "All right, Molly, your story checks out."

"Well, of course it does," I blurted out, startled. "What did you think, I hurt Erica?"

"Did you?" he asked.

"Of course not!" I stared at Drew, concerned by his blank expression.

He grimaced. "Right now, I don't believe anybody about anything. This mess is just getting worse and worse." His puppy eyes looked exhausted.

My heart sank. I could see Detective Lacey doubted me, but now Drew? How could he think I'd have anything to do with Erica's injury?

Lacey smiled a wry grin at Deputy Drew, her almond shaped eyes regarding him with familiarity. Was this more than a glance between colleagues? Just how familiar were these two? I felt an odd pang in my chest. Was I an idiot? Deputy Drew Powell and I weren't dating, so it was none of my business how familiar he was with Detective Lacey or any other women, for that matter. But it bothered me.

I had this high school-crush thing going on in my head. I'd have to hold my tongue when I drove to the hospital with him and avoid asking if he and Lacey were more than friends.

I stepped into the kitchen and washed my hands eagerly. I could use a firehose and bleach and still feel like I hadn't gotten my hands clean.

As I dried my hands I admired a crystal blue vase filled with three rainbow roses. I strained my neck to peek in the family room. The deputies and EMT were tending to Erica. I walked over to the flowers on the counter and picked up the business-size white card attached to the slender pink ribbon around the vase. The note read: *Thinking of you, your favorite baker.*

Impulsively, I removed the card and stuck it in my back pack leaving the top unzipped. I'd be needing the card if I was going to act as Erica in order to ask the florist who the delivery was from. The kaleidoscope of roses had been dyed so that each petal displayed a different vibrant hue of yellow, blue, green, purple and pink to create a flower arrangement that had to be unique to a specialty florist. It wouldn't be hard to find the florist that made the bouquet.

For a brief moment the thought of interfering with a police investigation crossed my mind, but the thought of being arrested outweighed my common sense. I needed to solve the case before they hauled me away. Plus, I wanted to verify my hunch that Erica's favorite baker could be one of the Doughty cousins. Would their jealousy or anger at Jim be enough of a motive to poison him? But why would one of the Doughty cousins harm Erica? My prying into the investigation gave me hope that the police would add someone else to the suspect list. It was no fun being on the list alone.

Snickers came over and nudged me with his nose and I patted his head.

Out of the blue, Detective Lacey walked into the kitchen and handed a treat to Snickers. A strange gesture, coming from the ice queen.

I softened when I saw her get down on one knee to pet him. But my suspicions rose when she pulled out another treat from a baggie and let Snickers eat it, and then lick the bag clean. Lacey swiped at Snickers' slobber.

"I'm sorry. He's a slobbery mess when it comes to Pup-peroni treats." I couldn't believe this was the same lady of steel that had berated me with questions a few minutes earlier. Why was she now being so nice to my dog?

Lacey smiled up at me. The bag of treats were gone, and instead the plastic was lined wet with dog slobber. "Come here Snickers." I reached for my backpack to retrieve a Kleenex to wipe Snickers' jowls. When I grabbed the handle, it turned upside down dumping the contents onto the floor. I saw Detective Lacey's eyebrows rise.

I looked at the pile on the floor. No gun or knife came tumbling out, just a mixture of wallet, keys, Snickers candy bar, lip balm, my moleskin notebook, loose coins... rubber gloves and a mask!

Silence filled the tiny kitchen.

"Okay," I finally said aloud. "Okay." I crouched down to quickly gather up the items tossing them in backpack.

"What do you have here?" Lacey poked at the mask with a pen.

"Hey, I know what this looks like. But it's nothing at all."

"Well, it sure doesn't look good." Her voice was quiet, but a smirk formed on her lips.

"I always carry gloves and a mask, just in case I plan to tend to a mint garden." Even though I said the words, I realized how shallow the excuse sounded.

Lucky walked into the kitchen and looked at the collection of my personal items spilled on the floor. When he eyed the gloves and mask his expression looked like I was carrying a weapon of mass destruction around in my backpack.

He gave me a look that said, *now you really have some explaining to do, Lucy.*

So much for dating a cop.

When life gives you lemons, trade them for coffee.
~ Anonymous

CHAPTER SIXTEEN

Erica wasn't allowed visitors yet at the hospital, so I agreed to meet Drew at the station for my statement. I had to stop by the Bean and check on my employees and talk to them about Erica. But first I needed a shower.

I stepped into the warm water and let it run over me. It felt like it would take every drop of hot water in my apartment and a lot of soap to get the blood off of me.

I blow dried my hair, got dressed in clean black leggings and a long-sleeved T-shirt, and then went in search of food.

I hadn't eaten since lunch at the Grille and had expended a lot of energy being terrified. I opened the refrigerator and stared at the empty shelves. A plastic baggie contained a few shriveled-up grapes, and my veggie drawer held one apple, one orange, and a few spotty carrots.

Even my freezer which usually held an endless supply of chocolate, including a bag of miniature Snickers, was bare.

"Let's go to the Bean," I said to Snickers.

I pulled my cell phone out of the charger on the counter, and bummer, discovered it hadn't been plugged into the socket. The battery barely had juice.

I smiled at my Charlie Brown Christmas tree I had bought at the grocery store a few days ago. The tree was lit with one strand of bright white lights, half a dozen colorful glass bulbs and silver tinsel. There were no presents under it yet.

Ugh. I had presents to wrap, a surprise visit from my mom to deal with, and a murder to solve.

As I walked to the café, I worried about having to make a police statement. When you find yourself invited to a police station interrogation room again for the second time in a few days, a word to the wise: it may be time to talk to a lawyer.

"Welcome back," Aurora said when I entered the café.

I strode over to the group, which consisted of Aurora, Bales, Chris, and even Granny Dee. There were hugs all around.

"Do you think whoever killed Jim also attempted to kill Erica?" Aurora blurted out.

"The police don't know details yet. I'm going to meet them in a few to tell them what I know." I hoped that I was only going to give a statement and I was not a suspect. Otherwise, I'd need to find a good criminal attorney. I thought I'd ask Granny if she could recommend one, just in case. I never had a need for one in the past. After all, I was a coffee shop owner. Even if my granddad had a lawyer, he'd probably not handle murder suspects. *Maybe I should text Aunt Tammera before I meet Drew at the Palma County station and get her advice on whether I needed to retain counsel or not.*

"This is all so terrible," Bales said.

"Who would do this?" Chris asked, his arms folded across his chest.

Aurora had a concerned look on her face as she twiddled with the strap of her apron. I moved toward her and gave my friend a hug in an attempt to diffuse the worried look on her face.

"Don't worry, the Palma County detectives are all over this," I said.

"Hmmp," Granny said. "That does little good in getting this settled once and for all. What can we do to help?"

"We can't go sticking our noses in everyone's business. We need to let them do their jobs." I said this in front of my crew, but deep down I needed help from Granny and Aurora.

The front door chimed, and several young couples came in the shop. "Bales and Chris, why don't you go help them? Make sure to offer the bake goods half price at this hour. And if you don't mind, can I get a sandwich please? I missed dinner tonight."

The two left to help the customers, leaving Granny, Aurora and me sitting in the kitchen. "Can we plan an emergency meeting at Granny's house tomorrow?" I trusted these two women in front of me more than anyone else in Bay Isles. "If we are to find out who did this, I'll need your help."

Granny narrowed her eyes at me. "I thought you said we were letting the police handle this."

I nodded toward my other two employees and whispered, "I need your help, but don't want everyone in Bay Isles to know."

"You need to be careful, my dear," Granny whispered back, placing her hand on mine. "If you would have shown up at Erica's house a few minutes earlier ... well, I shudder to think of you in danger, sweetie."

"I'll be fine," I said. But as I thought about it, how dangerous was this person? I figured one murderer and another attempt at murder meant he was dangerous indeed, assuming both Jim's death and Erica's injury were related. The police had said that nothing was disturbed at her house, so it wasn't a random burglary.

"You know who's behind this, don't you?" Granny asked.

"I have an idea and a few suspects I need to eliminate to narrow down my list," I answered. I was far from the truth, with only a handful of clues. Good clues. Some I hesitated to share with anyone yet, including Deputy Drew.

"That's my girl. Oh, and your Aunt Tammera called me a few minutes ago with an update," Granny said with a wry smile.

"You knew?" I couldn't hide anything from the McFadden side of the family.

"Of course, dear. I talk to all my daughters regularly."

"What was her message?" I asked, also wondering if she knew about my mom's surprise visit.

"She said yes to your first question, no to the second, and …" Granny frowned. "Oh, what was the last thing? Hmmm …"

Her forehead folded into a creased frown and her eyes rolled up and down, as if trying to remember something. Her fingers tapped on the arm of the chair. "Oh dear," Granny shrugged.

"What was the last thing?" I chewed on my tongue to stop me from saying anything more smart-alecky. I was grateful that she could help, but I needed all of Aunt Tammera's information.

"Well, anyway. I'll let you know when she calls back, dear. She had some Holiday Gala at the museum and said she'd call me tomorrow." The frown formed again but then her eyes twinkled as if the memory was almost right there. "Please keep in mind, sweetie, that my memory is a bit shoddy these days. So, if I remember two out of the three things, well, that's good. And if it's going to get you all bent out of shape, you might want to take your own messages next time."

I wanted to check my messages on my cell, but realized I had no charge. I guess it could wait.

"I just knew Erica had nothing to do with Jim's death," Aurora said. "But who would do this?"

"Have you checked out Mayor Clawson?" Granny whispered under her breath.

"The mayor?" I knew he had fished with Jim Grist. In fact, half of Bay Isles' fishermen had at one time or another.

"Yes. Seems he was really upset about the fishing contest. He felt his son and his partner should have won, and Jim broke the rules. But no one could prove it."

"I hardly think cheating in a fishing tournament would be a motive ..." I stopped. "...especially premeditated murder." Mayor Clawson was a large sturdy man with a deep tan that set off his silver locks. If he gained ten more pounds, wore wire-rimmed glasses, and grew a snow-white beard, he could double for Santa.

Now the Mayor's son, Todd, on the other hand, I had been seen behind Gator's Bait and Tackle the night before the murder. Could he have been upset over the fishing tournament loss?

"If he was upset and hit him on the head or something, that's more an act of ..." Granny rubbed her chin. "...that's a crime of passion. Since this guy was poisoned, someone had to plan it. And the killer left him on the beach like a bloated mackerel to make it look like an accident."

Granny Dee surprised me. She couldn't remember what Aunt Tammera had told her ten minutes ago about Jim and Erica, but she could remember murder motives.

She must have seen my quizzical expression, because she added, "I've watched a lot of Murder She Wrote episodes."

I nodded. "Well, whoever did this hasn't lived here very long."

"Why?" Aurora asked.

"For one, they didn't know the tides," I blurted out.

"We didn't find the body, so explain?" Granny said very interested.

"I will tomorrow when we meet. I'm tired and I still need to go meet Drew at the station for a statement. Bring your list of suspects and motives, and I don't care if it's Santa ringing the bell at the marina. We need to gather everything we have. We can't rest until this person is caught. And we need to find out soon, before it puts a damper on our Holly Fest."

I left them to think about that and headed toward the front of the café. I greeted a few customers and did what I loved best—I made a few lattes. My gingerbread, eggnog and chai flavors are all spice based and make a fantastic combination, that is, if my customer wanted a taste of the holidays in one cup. The secret ingredients made a winner of a drink.

"Do you want a surprise?" I asked the young lady who was still milling over the chalkboard menu of drinks.

"Yes, surprise me. I'd like a cold one, please." Her eyes twinkled as she smiled at her friends.

"Are you allergic to anything? And do you like raspberry?" I loved to experiment, and this drink I had in mind was one I had made for my staff and friends from time to time.

After we discussed the drink, I went to work and made a combination of white mocha, raspberry, and eggnog. The concoction tastes amazing together and made for a great holiday feel. Served in a clear glass, it came out frosty red and white striped and had the sweetness of the iced white chocolate, a bit of tart from the raspberry syrup and the beloved taste of eggnog.

"This is delicious," the customer proclaimed. "Thank you."

I resumed my drifting about the café, talking to customers and making a few drinks. This was fun, and I was getting paid.

After wolfing down a sandwich and stalling for thirty minutes, it was time to make my way to the Palma County Sheriff's Department. Aurora said she'd watch Snickers until I returned.

I caught Aurora before I left. "Come with me," I said. She followed me into the office, and once we were alone I asked, "Hey, you don't know a Missy who works at the Grille, do you?"

"Hmm," Aurora scratched her chin. "You don't mean Mistletoe?"

"Mistletoe? Is that a girl's name? Is she a bartender at the Tiki Hut on Friday nights?"

"Yes. She was born on Christmas, like you. She's a lot older though. I think she's …"

"I don't care about her age," I interrupted. "Do you know how I can talk to her before Friday night?"

"I can check and leave you a text," Aurora said as she bent over a large shopping bag on the office floor.

"Here." She pulled a blue top out of the Macy's shopping bag.

"What's this?" I asked, puzzled.

"Consider it my early Christmas gift to you."

"I can't take your shirt!"

"Yes, you can. You can return it if you like or keep it. You're going to see Drew, right?

"It's not a dinner date, it's a witness statement. And besides what's wrong with my

206

…," I looked down and saw a brown colored shirt over black leggings and stopped talking.

"This is a Free People cold shoulder top. Besides, with your eyes, you'll look great in cosmic blue," she bubbled.

"Cosmic what?"

"Just shut up and put on the blue top," she said as she closed the door to the tiny office.

I did as instructed, and I had to say that the blouse fit perfectly. While I straightened the top, Aurora took off her high-heeled black half boots and said, "Give me your ballet flats."

"No," I protested.

She pushed me in a chair and her dark eyes flared at me. She bent down and tugged at my shoes.

"All right. All right," I said. "But you're a half size smaller than me."

"It will be fine for an hour. Take your flats with you if you want. I have a pair of Keds in my car."

I nodded. I had a stop to make before coming back to the café, and I had a feeling I should wear my flats in case I needed to run.

Blessed. Well Dressed & Coffee Obsessed.
~ Anonymous

CHAPTER SEVENTEEN

When I came out of the office with Aurora, Granny took a look at my updated outfit and nodded her approval.

Why was I stalling to go to the police station?

I placed my empty sandwich plate in the sink, grabbed my backpack off the counter, and made my way to the front door with Granny following closely at my borrowed heels. She held a cup of flour as she waddled, without a cane, behind me.

"I'm just saying be careful what you tell them. I know you have a good idea about Jim's murderer, and before Erica was injured you were her ticket to exoneration," Granny said.

She watched way too many police shows. But she was right, I had enough clues in my notebook and a good idea what needed to be done to clear Erica, me, or any of my baristas of the murder of Jim Grist. I had a few more people to talk to, and then I would tell Drew everything.

Speaking of handsome Drew, I heard Snickers bark and a familiar voice. I stopped abruptly and turned to take my backpack to the office. I collided with Granny. She tossed a half cup of the flour on my cosmic blue shirt and my face. I stepped back, inhaling flour fumes, only to collide with Deputy Drew, whose face was now inches from mine.

"Yikes," Granny yelped.

Instinctively, Drew grabbed my waist to keep me from falling back into Granny. We were so close. All I had to do was lean in and we'd be close enough to be kissing. But I didn't. We held in that position for a few seconds, a fiery energy linking us together.

"Now look at this mess!" Granny's shrill voice interrupted our moment.

I felt my cheeks burn red under a coating of flour.

"You guys look cozy," Aurora said, coming up behind us.

I jumped away from Drew and turned to face Aurora and Granny. Aurora grinned at me. She looked between Drew and me like she thought she'd almost interrupted us about to smooch. *Were we?*

I turned to stare at him. I was pretty sure that wasn't a happy smile on his face. I glared back at Aurora.

"Sorry, I sent Deputy Drew back here. He said he needed to talk to you," Aurora said with a shrug. *Did she just wink at me?*

"I was just on my way to the police station for a statement," I said to Drew.

"Can we talk here?" he asked

"Sure, what's up," I managed to say.

Aurora returned to the front of the café while Granny scurried about cleaning up the flour. She stopped and asked, "Are you here on official police business, or is this a social call?" Granny stared at Drew as he brushed flour from his shirt.

"Granny, you know he doesn't make social calls in uniform," I said snidely.

"Then what can we do for you, deputy?" Granny snorted.

"You can call me Drew," he said, trying to smile, but not quite there. "I need to talk to you," he said, turning his attention to me.

"What's up?" I asked nervously.

"You weren't snooping around at Jim's house, were you?" Drew asked.

I averted my eyes. *What? He sure was direct and to the point.* I glanced at Granny, but she kept her head down sweeping.

"Snooping? Do you think I would hang around a dead guy's house? I already said I didn't know the guy." I needed to hand my backpack to Granny because it contained my notebook and all my *snooping* notes.

"We were checking out your mint garden theory. You had a point about the mint the other day. And some elderly lady in Jim's neighborhood said I had been the second person to ask about a mint garden. I just thought you'd be the one asking, even though she couldn't remember the woman very well. She said the lady was older and married." He looked me up and down.

I felt proud of Connie not blowing my cover. *Sweet lady. I'll have to take her cupcakes when this is all over.*

"Mint garden?" I asked, not looking him in the eye.

"Mo, I don't know what you have brewing, and I don't want to know, just so you're not snooping around in my case."

I sighed. "I want to help, so I can't guarantee I won't interfere"

Drew narrowed his eyes at me. "Tell me you aren't talking to suspects. And you're not hiding anything from me?"

What could I say to distract him? "Well I know I'm not hiding a secret garden out back." I pointed to the far end of the kitchen toward the back door, where the exit to the boardwalk led.

I suppose it was an instinctive ploy, for when Drew turned to look, I passed my backpack to Granny.

She took it and turned toward the front of the café. Luckily, Drew hadn't noticed the exchange.

When he turned back he said, "Uh-huh. I just wanted to make sure this neighbor hadn't seen you at Jim's house asking around."

I folded my arms and glared at him. The effect might have been more intimidating if it hadn't been for all the flour on my face. I probably looked like Casper the Friendly Ghost.

"Can I have a look around?" he asked.

Granny had returned to the kitchen sans my backpack, which was now probably being tossed in Aurora's car. I felt guilty, for I had nothing to hide, but my clues in my notepad would look suspicious. And besides, I still had a few unanswered questions I want to investigate on my own. I had a theory, or more of a hunch at this point, but I still didn't want Deputy Drew Powell and his team to intercept my hunches.

"You don't have a warrant, as far as I can tell," Granny said. "This is Mo's business, and if you come in here with allegations about poisons hidden here, it could cost her customers and close the café down in a New York minute."

Something flickered across his face. Curiosity? Anger?

"We don't intend to cause any harm to her business, Mrs. McFadden."

"Dee, dear." Granny patted Drew's hand. "Call me Dee."

He turned to me. "Mo, it wouldn't hurt to have a look. And we can have a warrant here in an hour." He flushed from the collar of his Palma County Sheriff shirt to the top of his hairline when he mentioned the warrant.

I looked at Granny for advice. I was well aware of Deputy Drew's eyes on me instead, but I couldn't look at him. My cheeks were burning again, but this time I felt guilty.

Drew raised an eyebrow at me.

I grinned at the rose-colored officer and said, "Let me clean my face and we can talk."

While in the café bathroom, I looked in the mirror and did a double take. I took stock of my appearance in the mirror. Never had I looked so fair and fragile. My pale skin had almost a porcelain quality, and, well the flour hadn't helped the look. While my ginger hair was blown-dried tame, the tendrils were wavy. Dark circles were gathering under each eye.

I was tired and needed my bed. My brain was in a pre-caffeinated fog. What did handsome Drew want to talk to me about here? Were these the questions he said he had to ask me before when he

wanted to meet at my apartment?

I scrubbed my face, starting with removing the flour around my eyes. I looked at my reflection. "Great now I look like a reverse raccoon."

I ran a brush through my hair and walked out of the bathroom. Drew sat stone-faced and silent at a table, arms crossed. *Well, this is going to be fun,* I thought.

Aurora seemed to be dancing a nervous little jig as she approached the table. Granny moved behind the counter and watched from a safe distance.

"Do you want a latte?" I asked, as Aurora placed a cup of coffee in front of me.

He nodded. Aurora smiled brightly at him, and before turning she winked at me.

214

"You know my partner, Deputy Ted, is very anxious to solve this case. He's retiring at the end of the year," Drew said.

"I get it. He wants to solve it before he retires. Who wouldn't want to leave a clean desk behind when he hangs up the badge?" I swirled my stir stick in my cup, mixing up the cinnamon floating on the top.

"Exactly."

"But there seems to be a lot of people who may have wanted Jim dead," I said, looking him in

those clear, blue eyes.

"But you need to stay out of it, Mo." He looked concerned. "You'll wind up in more trouble."

"From what you're not saying to me, it looks like I'm already in trouble. I'm a murder suspect, right?" I asked. "I don't know how it can get worse than that."

"I'm just saying, you don't need to be poking your nose around in our investigation."

"You're not denying I'm a suspect?"

"I don't think for one minute that you are."

"Then why ask around town about me?"

He looked surprised. "I get it. A small community, everyone knows everyone's business. We're eliminating everyone. And you have to admit, you found the body, you grow mint, Granny's cane marks—or someone's cane marks—in the sand … and there's more that points to this café, at least. And more specifically, you and …," he paused, "… and Snickers."

"Snickers? Surely you can't think because me and my dog found the body …"

"… and Erica."

"Okay I give you that, but come on, me?" I looked at Snickers sunning on the porch. "Us?"

He nodded.

Aurora returned and placed a latte in front of him, and a plate of pastries between us. I noticed the fresh pink frosted cupcakes and thought about my stop later tonight.

When Aurora left the book nook, I asked Drew, "Who else do you have?"

Lucky shrugged. "We had been looking at his on-again-off-again girlfriend."

My heart thudded. Did he mean Erica? I nodded like I knew who he was talking about. I had a good idea anyway. At least he was talking to other suspects.

"My barista?" I asked.

Lucky didn't say anything, so I figured it was her he was talking about. I waited, hoping I could outlast him. I did.

He took a sip of his latte. "Some of your customers saw them arguing the day before his body was found."

So, they already knew about the argument. But they didn't know about Jim and Erica's marriage? But wouldn't she now be ruled out? I did know that neither Jim or Erica had mint gardens at their houses.

I nibbled on a blueberry muffin. It was late, and I felt a huge relief not to be going to the station. But that relief only lasted a few minutes, until I saw Detective Lacey and her partner show up.

Lacey had that look in her eye. It was the same one she had at Erica's house.

Drew and I discussed Erica's prognosis, while Detective Lacey placed her coffee order. Her partner had gotten a call and stepped outside to take it.

"Thank goodness, she'll be okay," I said to Drew at Erica's update. "When can I see her?"

"She's having memory problems right now. She can't even remember who hit her or where she was at the time of the injury, and all."

"Poor girl," I nodded.

"Well, well, here we are again," Lacey said, walking up to me and Drew. "We're here on police matters, if you're willing to talk here." She pointed at an empty seat. "You've already been to the police station once in the past few days. You don't really want to make a second trip, do you?"

I shook my head and took my eyes away from her to Drew, and back at her. "Sure. Pull up a chair. I see no harm in speaking here." I felt relieved. How serious could it be if they wanted to chat here versus an interrogation room. Unless I was being the fool. Did this mean I was giving information freely without a lawyer? Maybe it would feel good to clear the air. And my employees and customers could see I was cooperating with the police, even collaborating with them.

It was evident after a few minutes, I was being a fool.

"Tell me again," Detective Lacey said. "You were checking on Erica because she missed work? And because she had an argument with the dead guy? What did they discuss?" She couldn't hold back her sneer.

"Yes, as I said for the third time, I was worried about her. Did you check her house? Did she have a garden?"

"I'll ask the questions here."

"I already explained that I didn't know what she had argued with Jim over. I went to her house because I was worried about her. Do you have her cell phone, and did you check it? You can see my worried text and voice messages."

"I'm not going to mention it again. We'll ask the questions." Detective Lacey rolled her eyes.

"Oh, sorry."

We went around and around with the same questions and my same answers.

Each time I told my story, I remembered new pieces of information. I recalled the coffee pot had been left on. I remembered the texts I had sent her.

I had been told that when a suspect—*was I a suspect?* — was telling their alibi, they didn't tell the exact same story each time. If the person is telling the truth, it would be the same answer, but with additional information recalled as the story was repeated. This was the case of my responses today. I kept with the truth. I had been there to check on Erica. The fact that I wanted to see if she had a mint garden or a wheelbarrow in her garage, I had omitted from this conversation.

It did feel good to clear the air. I discussed everything. Well almost everything. I ignored the voice of common sense that should have prompted me to confide in Deputy Drew a day ago. I told them about Erica and Jim's marriage, and how she wanted a divorce. I told them about the Mayor's son and the fisherman that were upset over the contest money. And the allegations of Jim cheating to win. I didn't tell them I had already spoken to the Mayor's son and that he had a solid alibi. I'd let them chase that.

I even told them about the surveillance tapes from the bridge, which they already knew about.

"So you knew what vehicles were on and off the bridge between those hours before the bridge got stuck in the up position?" Detective Lacey asked again.

"Yes, like I said, I have a friend who let me look at the tapes." I wasn't going to let them know Aurora had led me to the drawbridge operator.

"Well, then you wouldn't mind coming to the station to look at the tapes with us and help identify the vehicles you know?"

"Sure, I can do that."

Detective Lacey stopped and read through notes in a small ratty spiral pad. "Didn't you dislike Jim?" Detective Lacey threw at me.

"Who said that?" I had no idea who would have said that. "I really didn't know him."

"Can you just answer the question? I understand that after Jim spoke with Erica, you banned him from the café?"

220

I nodded. I had told my employees that he wasn't allowed inside the café. But who would have told the police that?

"Why was that? Just because he had words with Erica?" Her eyes narrowed at me.

Drew turned away.

"Jim's a man of many words, most of them containing four letters. And since he always found it difficult to omit the colorful language, I had to ban him from entering the café. His buddies can come in and buy his coffee, but he needs to drink it outside."

"And he never approached you about this?"

"No. I just suggested it the other day. I hadn't seen him since. I never got the opportunity to tell him because, well then, he showed up, um, on the beach."

"Isn't it true you left Erica off the schedule this week, *before* she was injured?"

"Yes. But that's because she hadn't called in." How had she reviewed my baristas work schedule?

Detective Lacey leaned forward, one elbow resting on the table, her face inches from mine, "We're getting a warrant to search the café and your apartment."

"What?" My chest tightened and my palms
became sweaty.

"We found a napkin on Jim's body." She stopped for effect. Before Detective Lacey could pick up one of our white napkins stamped with our brown logo, I knew what she was going to say. "It was *your* napkin."

I gulped in air, but it didn't seem to reach my lungs.

Drew handed me a glass of water. I waved it away. "But his body was found outside Addicted to the Bean, and that napkin could have blown there from anyone leaving our café."

"No, I said it was *your* napkin," Detective Lacey said. "And it was stuck to a Velcro strap on his fishing vest. Forensics thinks it adhered there while the victim was moved to the beach."

The air in the café felt stifling as I tried to digest her words. Why would my café napkin make me a suspect?

"The contents of the napkin had coffee stains on it." Detective Lacey pointed to the napkin sitting under my coffee cup.

"So? That could be from anyone that comes in here."

"The coffee stains had been analyzed."

"And?"

"And, it was yours. Can you tell me how that got on the body?"

"That's ridiculous. What do you mean mine? How can you tell it was *mine*?"

She pointed a finger at my cup of coffee. "Coffee with low-fat milk, sweetener and cinnamon, right?"

I nodded, shooting a glance at Drew. The look on Drew's face made my hair stand on end.

"A perfect match to the stains all over the napkin," Detective Lacey said.

The room spun. Where did they get this information? I looked at Drew again. Had he told her how I took my coffee? Was our date at the Bridgeport Falls Brew house only a set up?

Here I was analyzing my customers by the kind of coffee they drank. But the cops were doing one better. They were analyzing the kind of coffee I drank to pin a murder on me!

"But, but, anyone can take their coffee that way," even as I said the words it sounded shallow.

"I understand that. But when you combine that with the other stains on the napkin, it really narrows it down."

"Other stains?"

"The other stains we retrieved from the napkin were a perfect match to Snickers' slobber."

Was that a smirk she hid behind her coffee cup?

A small breath escaped my lips. My fingers felt cold against my cheeks and the room was spinning. "But, that can't be ..."

Before I could utter another word, the café door jingled. An older, large man with gray hair in a white shirt, red and blue striped tie and black suit pants entered. He walked over to our table and said, "This conversation is over."

"And you are?" Detective Lacey asked.

"I'm Duncan Clawson, Miss Brewster's lawyer." He produced a card and handed it to Lacey.

Lacey shrugged. "Just so you know, we've applied for a warrant to search *your client's* business and home," she said as she stood up.

Mr Duncan Clawson shrugged his meaty shoulders.

I exhaled with relief. I honestly didn't know the man in front of me, but I knew Aunt Tammera had gotten Granny's message.

Detective Lacey and her crew turned to walk out. Drew avoided my eyes.

Lacey turned toward me and said, "Don't leave town."

Duncan Clawson showed her his best smile.

Caffeine made me do it. ~ Anonymous

CHAPTER EIGHTEEN

I stood on the café porch and watched Deputy Drew Powell drive away, wondering if this would be the end of our budding relationship. Of course, it would. He was an officer of the law and I was a possible murder suspect.

Back in the café, my employees gawked at me.

"Well, that was interesting," Aurora said, breaking the ice.

"Thank you, Mr. Clawson," I said to Duncan. "Orange isn't my best color."

"Call me DC. And don't you worry, you'll never see the inside of a cell," he said.

"Did Aunt Tammera send for you?" I asked.

Granny gathered closer. I noticed she had on her shawl, and that indicated she was ready to leave.

"No, who's that?" DC answered.

"Who called you?" I was puzzled how DC knew the cops were here talking to me.

"I got a call from my brother, Mayor Clawson," he grinned.

"Of course, now I recognized your name. You two are brothers? But how'd the mayor know?" I could see DC's resemblance to our town mayor.

"He said someone at the Palma County Sheriff's Department told him about your so-called meeting here tonight, and that you might need a lawyer." DC took a sip of the Bay Isle's House Blend coffee Aurora had prepared for him.

"Well, who could that be?" I said out loud, but I knew it could only have been one person: Deputy Drew. I smiled. Maybe there was hope in our relationship after all.

"Maybe you need to get friendlier with the handsome Deputy Lucky and find out who he has on his suspect list. Besides you, I mean." Aurora smiled.

I felt my stomach clench when I realized I was still the main suspect. I wondered if the deputies knew that one of the Doughty cousins had a crush on Erica? That could have placed them on the suspect list for Jim's murder as a jealous lover, but that didn't explain Erica's injuries. Aurora was right, I'd have to work faster to clear myself before their list of suspects whittled down to just one suspect – me!

Aurora mistook my silence as I was lost in thoughts. "Sorry, I was only teasing," she said, touching my arm lightly.

I nodded. My friends were there to help me, and this was no time to feel sorry for myself.

"I'll need to meet with you tomorrow," DC said. "And think of who would set you up with this evidence they have against you and Snickers." DC stared over the top of his cup while we all stood around the front counter.

"Set me up?" It hadn't occurred to me until that moment.

Aurora and Granny leaned in.

Bales called Snickers inside and shut the door, and then flipped the sign to *closed*. It wasn't quitting time, but I had agreed to close early tonight. We were all exhausted from the excitement of the news of Erica's attempted murder. The extended stay of the police cars out front had caused the Bay Isles residents to gather and gawk.

"Yes, dear," Granny said. "Don't you see it? Someone has made sure you are the main suspect. The mint, the napkin with your coffee ingredients, Snickers' saliva, and even where the body was dumped behind your apartment and the café."

I rolled my eyes. "Why would someone want to frame me?"

"Because the real murderer wants you to take the fall," Aurora said.

"Listen to us, sweetie," Bales put her hand on mine. "You need to be careful. There's a dangerous murderer out there running loose. He's killed one person and attempted to kill another."

"She's right," DC said. "You need to watch your back."

"The police have to see it's a setup, don't they? What motive could I have? And how would I have gotten poison?"

"Your grandmother was a nurse," DC said.

"A hundred years ago," I replied. "No offense, Granny."

"None taken, my dear. Come stay with me and Henrietta tonight and get some rest. And stop trying to figure this out. We can meet tomorrow and discuss our lists of possible suspects and then you can meet with DC."

Everyone said their goodbyes and there were hugs all around, except for jolly DC. He took a bag of pastries and snuck out the back door to avoid some gawkers who still lingered outside.

Aurora had been perched on a stool. She jumped down and mentioned to me to follow her to the back office.

"I have something for you," Aurora said. She reached in her purse and pulled out a silver and green flash drive. "Here," she said, holding it out.

"What's this?"

"I asked Tony the Ten-Cent bridge tender keeper if I could have a look at the camera shots from that night."

"And he let you take copies of the photos?"

"He conveniently went to make a cup of coffee while I looked at the photos and copied them."

"I love you," I said, jumping up and planting a kiss on her cheek.

"Wait until you see the photos first from that night before you profess your love for me."

"What? Are they useable?"

"Maybe a few, but for the most part the photos are blurry."

The suspense was killing me, and if I had time I would have looked myself. "Did any stand out?"

She thought for a moment. "From the looks of the photos, there were a lot of black and white cars that drove on and off the island that night." She grinned.

"The photos are black and white?" I was disappointed.

"Yes. But the black cars are distinguishable from other colors even through the grainy exposures. More than half were black cars."

Everyone I knew had a black car. I often drove Grandpa's black Saab. Aurora had a black Mazda. Erica drove a black Honda Civic. And Jet, Granny's gardener drove a black SUV. I'd even seen Detective Lacey driving a black mid-sized SUV the morning I discovered Jim's body.

I hated to admit it but the photos on the bridge that night may not give us any clues. And besides the bridge access, I still had boats to consider. But without a dock on the bay side of the beach, and the low tides it would have taken a paddle board or canoe-type water vessel to carry a body to the beach.

"There was one truck that I saw twice. Both coming to and leaving Bay Isles over the bridge."

"Truck? Like a pickup truck?"

"No. It was a delivery truck."

"Delivery?"

"Yup. The Doughy Delight delivery truck. I recognized their logo even though the photos were blurry."

I rubbed my chin. I thought about Felix's comment about Erica that morning.

"What are you thinking?" Aurora asked.

"I'm thinking if any delivery truck had the right to cross over the bridge it would be theirs. The Doughty cousins live here on Bay Isles and their pastry shop is in Bridgeport." Plus, they made early morning deliveries around Bay Isles. My search for alternative suspects was leading nowhere fast. "Do you recall ever seeing Erica with Felix or Jack?"

"No. Other than hanging out at Smuggs."

"Smuggs?"

"The after-hour dive bar. Smuggs as it's known to the locals, but its full name is Smugglers Tavern. Rumor has it that Smuggs was named after the smugglers that were shipwrecked on the island."

"I get it. The smugglers were stranded here, so they opened a bar and sold legitimate liquor where people with parrot tattoos could drink and eat pizza."

Aurora smiled. "Something like that. It does attract the younger population. They serve low priced drinks and stay open until early morning hours. It hits the bifecta for criteria for the younger crowd at bars in Bay Isles."

"I'm pretty sure bifecta isn't a word."

"Well if it was a word, Smuggs is –,"

"– I get it. Where's Smuggs?"

"Tucked behind the deli. The owner also has a place in Bridgeport. Dead Bobs."

"Dead Bobs? Let me guess, the bar's named after a dead relative named Bob?"

She smiled and nodded. "If you haven't noticed there isn't an abundance of younger people around here. So yes, Jack has been seen with Erica from time to time, but that's because the younger group seems to hang together."

"At Dead Bobs and Smuggs." I sighed.

I was disappointed that the photos hadn't revealed much. "Thanks for this," I held up the thumb drive, then slipped it into the side pocket of my backpack. "I still have a few stops to make."

"Let me know if I can help in any way." Aurora reached into her purse and pulled out a Snickers bar. "Emergency sugar supply," she said, pressing it into my hand. "Be careful."

I nodded. We exchanged hugs and I left the office to get Granny and Snickers.

Twenty minutes later I dropped Granny and Snickers off at her house and promised to sleep at her place after my errand.

When I went to exchange the Oldsmobile for the Saab, I knew I needed to check out the gardening shed. I was curious about whether the wheelbarrow had any evidence of sand on the tires. I turned on the flashlight, deciding to leave the shed interior light off in order not to draw attention to my task.

I searched by shining the beam up and down the rows of clay pots, bags of potting soil, and the dusty and dirty garden tools. The shed was so full that I had to climb over a few half whiskey barrels to get to the back. I tripped over a rake and sent a pile of porcelain urns crashing. If that didn't wake up the neighborhood, I don't know what would. I used a stack of gardening magazines as a step stool to look on the top shelves.

The air held a musky, moldy smell. As a precaution, I pulled a paper garden mask off a hook and covered my nose and mouth with it.

There were plenty of items in the shed that could have been used as a weapon for Erica's injury. Drew had said it was a blunt object that had caused the injury, but the weapon wasn't found at the scene. There were pruning shears with heavy handles, shovels, trowels, hoes, and even a large saw, but no wheelbarrow. None of these items could have been used by me or anyone in our household as a murder weapon, because a thick layer of dirt and grime covered them, and they were clearly undisturbed for months. I searched further, and there in the corner was the wheelbarrow. Unlike everything else in the shed covered with cobwebs, it looked shining clean. Too clean. Wouldn't Jet routinely use it?

Before I could check out the tires, I heard footsteps. I whirled around and saw Jet staring at me. I felt my face flush red with guilt, but in the glow of the flashlight he seemed not to notice.

"Can I help you find something, Miss Molly?" Jet asked with enough sarcasm in his voice to cause a chill.

"No, I was just looking for something," I replied.

"Well, did you find it?"

"I think I did." I reached for a pair of pruning shears.

He eyed the shears. "Is that all?"

"Yes, thank you." I felt a shudder run down my back when I turned and walked out of the shed past Jet's glaring eyes.

I decided against driving the Saab to Felix's neighborhood. Instead, I took the golf cart. In my rush I had forgotten to change back into my flats. This was a dangerous proposition, driving a golf cart and using spiked heels to accelerate.

After a jerky start, I reached his street and turned off the golf cart lights. I cruised by several houses, packed in closely, until I spotted what I was looking for—the Doughy Delight pastry truck.

I parked the golf cart and managed to creep up the sidewalk without stumbling. My heels made more noise than a mariachi band as I clicked up the driveway. There were no lights in the house. I peered in the driver's side door of the truck, and it was unlocked. If I opened the door, would it activate the alarm? It was a risk I could take. But after my recent run in with the law, I decided to check out back first.

Quietly, I began creeping around Felix's backyard. I should have brought Snickers. That way, instead of being taken for a peeping Tom, I could look like a neighbor in search of her lost dog.

It only took a few moments to realize that the large swimming pool in the postage-stamp sized backyard had left little room for grass or anything else green to grow.

Besides, Felix and his cousin Jack had a solid alibi for the night Jim had been poisoned. Both were attending the same AA meeting with a friend and were seen by two dozen people afterwards at the AA annual holiday party.

As I returned to the side yard, I noticed the latch to the gate of Felix's next-door neighbor's house was broken.

I stepped over to the gate to take a closer look. Sure enough, the latch needed repair. I eased myself closer and spotted several pieces of gravel that were disturbed and laying on the path leading to the gate. The path led from the front to the back of the house.

I switched on the flashlight, following the path to the neighbor's backyard. *Hmm,* I wondered. I couldn't see any lights out back. I gave the tall, wooden door a shove. It creaked open. I took one step in and shined the light at the plush garden. A pair of big, unblinking, round eyes stared back at me out of the darkness.

"Eeeek!" I shrieked, stumbling in my high heels head first. My heart pounded so hard it was a wonder the homeowners couldn't hear my ribcage rattle.

Once my heart stopped its stampeding, I realized the eyes I were staring at were those of a garden gnome.

A gnome? Sure enough, there stood a foot-high garden gnome with round bright eyes. On further inspection, the little guy was dressed in bright blue overalls and a red hat. His eyes and smile were so creepy, it's a wonder I hadn't doused him with my pepper spray.

Before I could shine my light away from the little man, I sneezed.

The back-porch light came on.

Time for my exit. I could imagine the resident chasing me down the driveway or calling the police.

I jumped up. My cheeks flushed from the encounter with the garden statue. It was mortifying to think the gnome had almost blown my cover.

As I hobbled painfully in the ill-fitting boots back to the golf cart, my nose itched, and I had to pinch it to keep from further sneezing.

It was fifteen minutes later when I stopped by the Grille.

By an off chance that Missy would be working the Tiki Bar, I wanted to stop in and ask her a few questions.

As luck would have it, she was on duty, and the little bar and patio were jammed with people.

I was exhausted, but at the same time filled with adrenaline. However, the last thing I wanted was a Rum Runner—alone. But a glass of red wine couldn't hurt and would help me sleep.

It took ten minutes before a bar-back could take my order and hand me a glass of red vino. I had nodded hello to Missy from across the rectangle-shaped bar. She acknowledged me, but she had been too busy with a group of bachelorettes to take my order or speak to me.

I swished the red wine in my glass, salivating at the thought of tasting it. In college, the beer-guzzling college guys I had dated couldn't tell a Zinfandel from a Cabernet. One of my Aunties, not Tammera, but Aunt Alice, had a knack for wine tasting. She had quite an investment in various California wines and had taught me a thing or two.

"There you are," I said to Missy, who was now standing across the bar from me. I swallowed a small sip of wine, enjoying the flavor.

"Hi, you're Mo, right? From the Bean?" Missy said.

I nodded. "Yes, nice to meet you."

Missy reached over the bar and plucked a leaf or something green out of my hair and handed it to me.

"Thanks." I stared at it. "I guess I don't rock that look."

"You wear it well, but if you're going to have a roll in the hay before you come out you might want to run a brush through your hair afterwards." Missy pulled another few leaves off the back of my head.

I nodded and shrugged.

"Aurora said you might stop by. What can I help you with?" Missy looked exhausted, with dark shadows under her eyes.

"I was wondering if you happened to know the name of the girl that Jim Grist was with?"

Missy wrinkled her nose with an expression of distaste. "Sorry, I'm running off my feet here," Missy pointed around the bar. "Can we catch up later?"

"Sure." I wrote down my cell number on a slip of paper from my notebook and handed it to her. Missy stuck the paper in her jean pocket.

"Can you text me when you're free? I wanted to see if you could remember anything about the woman you saw Jim with a few weeks ago," I whispered, hoping no one near heard our conversation.

She shrugged and wiped a damp dishrag on the sticky bar countertop as she talked. "Jim came in here all the time with his fishing buddies."

I knew about his fishing buddies and had even talked to a few. I was curious about the lady he'd been seen with. "Did you ever see him on a date?"

"With Jim?" She rubbed her chin. "There was the one I saw him with recently."

"What was her name?"

"I'm not sure of her name. But it wasn't like a thing, you know."

I blinked and wondered what a *thing* referred to. "You mean it wasn't a date?"

She looked around and then back at me. "Yeah, she wasn't his type. You know he liked — well, —he liked the younger women."

"What did she look like?"

"She was much too ancient for him, and an old fuddy-duddy."

"Fuddy, what?" As long as I had her attention now, I'd try to find out who the mysterious woman was.

"She was the kind of person who faded into the wallpaper a bit. Definitely not his type. They had a connection though. The way they talked, and their body language showed a familiarity to it."

"Had you seen them together before?"

She stopped and thought. "No, can't say that I had. I don't guess we ever will, with him dead and all." She frowned. "Oh, I don't like to speak ill of the dead." She looked over at a man holding up an empty glass.

"I need to get Chuck his whiskey." She pointed to the large man in a red floral Tommy Bahama shirt, glaring at her.

I tried to squeeze in one more question. "What was she wearing and …?"

Missy cut me off. "I got to run." She waved her hand and said, "I'll text you if I think of anything else."

I nodded.

Missy placed a clean glass on the bar. She looked up from her pour of whiskey and said, "A dancer's outfit."

I finished my glass of wine, paid my check and left a nice tip on the bar.

Great. Now I had a potential mint-growin'-photographer- dancer to look for.

Back at Granny's I slipped into a pair of pink flannel PJs, downed a glass of water to dilute my glass of wine, and then Snickers and I curled up in bed. After a few minutes of logging in my notebook what I had discovered, I felt I was closer to the murderer. With my dog resting contentedly at my feet and my red notebook on my lap, I fell fast asleep.

I woke in the middle of the night to the sound of Granny's Siamese cat purring loudly at my door.

"Shhh," I said to George when I opened the bedroom door. "You'll wake the whole house."

I went to the window and listened to the noises outside, trying to recall the sound I'd heard that night Jim was left on the beach. Most of the night noises I recognized. This wasn't a familiar sound, and I couldn't place it. But I knew I had heard it before. Where?

I went to the bathroom and glanced in the mirror before climbing back into bed. My normally clear eyes, the color of jade, were now bloodshot and puffy. I looked like a recovering alcoholic who'd fallen off the wagon and been on a three-day bender.

When both Snickers and George were re-settled in bed with me, I turned off the light and slept like the proverbial log for a few hours anyway.

Sleep is a symptom of caffeine deprivation.
~ Anonymous

CHAPTER NINETEEN

My eyes popped open after a few hours of sleep. As I lay in the dark and listened to the sweet animal snores, it made me feel safe and happy.

But was I safe with the killer still on the loose? In the eyes of Detective Lacey, I was her main suspect. Would she even look at others? Did Deputy Drew think I was guilty?

What were the odds that my DNA, well my coffee's DNA, was found on the body? And considering that the forensic resources barely existed in the Palma County Sheriff's office, how had they uncovered this so quickly?

Since I was awake anyway, I sat up in bed. Snickers and George barely stirred. I switched on the bedside lamp, threw back the quilt, and pulled my notepad from my backpack. I jotted down a new suspect: me.

Feeling a sense of heaviness in the pit of my stomach, I stared at the blank page. After my second visit from Detective Lacey, I knew I had to find Jim's killer—and fast. Even without a true motive, I was her prime suspect. Doesn't the law state that people were innocent until proven guilty? But in a small town like Bay Isles, the gossip could destroy my business in a heartbeat. If the locals decided I was a cold-blooded killer, they might very well decide to boycott my café.

What did the detectives know? Under the suspect name Molly Brewster, I listed:

- Found body on beach
- Mint stains on body, and has access to a mint garden
- No clear alibi for the evening of Jim's murder
- Found napkin with coffee stains that match my particular choice of coffee
- My dog's orange-tinted saliva stains
- My fingerprints on the body – I had touched it to take a pulse
- Found victim's soon-to-be ex-wife unconscious from a blow to the head

Even though I was probably their number one suspect, they were missing a motive and the murder weapon. But, that was true for all the suspects I had on my list, as well. I knew later today the police would shut down The Bean and search my café and my apartment for traces of cyanide. I had to find the killer before that happened.

Then there was the issue of carrying a body to the beach. I knew that based on the tides that night, Jim's body hadn't washed up on shore and the body hadn't been dumped from a boat. It had been placed on the beach.

How would Erica have gotten the body to the beach if she had poisoned Jim?

Before I left Erica's house, I had told Drew I was in search of cat food. Instead, I had peeked in her garage hunting for a wheelbarrow but found none. Was that why Deputy Drew showed up at her house so quickly? Was he there to investigate her as well?

My phone was dead, so it had been silent all night. It was so peaceful at Granny's house. Sitting in the still of the night, I glanced out to the garden and beyond that the sea.

Our garden was one of my most cherished heirlooms. In it were lilacs and peonies that my grandmother had planted. My mom and granny shared their forget-me-nots, which they claimed to have come from a great-grandmother. My grandfather planted the coral bells bushes, which were also known as the Molly bushes. He had said they were beautiful and trouble-free, just like his only granddaughter.

Granddad used to say with their intensely colorful blooms, Miss Molly was the queen of the summer garden, thriving in the hot climate and attracting butterflies and hummingbirds.

What would he think today? His Miss Molly was a murder suspect.

George interrupted my thoughts as he awoke and jumped up on my chest. I leaned back with the weight of the cat's body on me and pushed up against my queen headboard. I rocked back and forth. It squeaked. Then the thought came to me. It was an aha moment. The squeaking sound and the pressure from leaning back gave me the final clue I needed.

I had one more place to check in the morning, but I felt certain that I'd just found the killer. I clicked off the light and fell fast to sleep.

After a dreamless night, I woke up refreshed and recharged.

Both animals were gone from my bedroom, and I heard laughter coming from downstairs. I glanced at the clock and was shocked to see it was 9:30. *Why hadn't Henrietta awakened me? Was Aurora expecting me by now at the Bean?*

I splashed water on my face and was glad to see my eyes were no longer red, and the puffiness beneath them had gone down.

I felt ready to conquer the world and catch a murderer, but first I needed to change out of my pink flannels with yellow daisies on them.

After throwing on a pair of faded Levi jeans, flip flops, and a green t-shirt, and running a brush through my frizzy hair, I went in search of coffee, food, and the source of the laughter.

I found Granny, Aurora, and Henrietta in the kitchen drinking coffee and tea and chatting pleasantly with each other.

"Well, look who's finally up," Granny said.

"Good morning, ladies," I said.

"Good morning," they replied in unison.

The fact that Henrietta handed me a cup of coffee prepared the way I liked it, goes without saying.

I stared at the cup, thinking about the soiled napkin that Detective Lacey had said they found on the body, then looked up. "Anything new?"

"You tell us," Aurora said as she ran her sparkly blue fingernails through George's fur. I had to admit, even though I was a dog fan, George was a gentle giant of a cat that could steal anyone's heart.

"I think I know who the murderer is," I blurted out.

"Well, that's something at least," Granny commented, smirking.

"I know. But I'll need your help. Can you all be at The Bean around noon? I have a stop to make this morning." I plopped half of a blueberry muffin in my mouth, swallowing it like a starving Rottweiler might eat a chunk of steak.

Aurora gazed at me with an expression of concern. "You're not going to confront the killer, are you?"

I couldn't reply with my mouth full of the sticky muffin.

"It would be dangerous," Aurora persisted.

"I agree with Aurora," Granny said. "You should call Detective Handsome. It sounds like you've got something solid to tell him."

Did I? "I am starting to piece it all together, Granny. I guess I should tell him what I've learned since yesterday. Can I use your phone to call the Palma Sheriff's department?"

"Where's yours?" Aurora asked.

"It ran out of juice, and I left my charger at my apartment," I replied.

"You can borrow my charger." Aurora rustled through her large Michael Kors knockoff purse and pulled out an iPhone charger.

"Thanks. I'll return it when I meet you at the café at noon." I pulled my cell from my backpack and plugged it in. "You know what, this can wait. Instead of calling the station now, can you invite Deputy Drew to the café?"

Aurora nodded. "Okay, let's go over what we know and see if we come to the same conclusions."

"We know that the dead fisherman, Jim Grinch …" Granny said.

"Grist," I corrected her.

"I'm just saying, he was a three-decker sauerkraut and toadstool sandwich with arsenic sauce." Granny grinned. "He's a mean one, Mr. Grist."

"Cyanide poison, not arsenic," I smiled at the reference to the song about the Grinch.

"And the cyanide poison had mint in it?" Aurora asked.

I shook my head.

"Then what does the mint have anything to do with this?" Henrietta asked.

"He was near a mint patch." I knew we'd been through this before.

"Mint patch?" Aurora scrunched her brows together.

"He had some on his hands," I replied.

Henrietta , Granny, and I glanced out the kitchen window to Granny's backyard.

"Then how many people did he know who have gardens or plants?" Aurora asked. "Let's unearth the real killer."

I grinned at her pun.

"Exactly," Henrietta said.

"We can narrow that down. But then what? We can't search their cabinets for poison," Aurora said.

"I'm pretty sure they wouldn't leave the murder weapon in their cabinets." Granny shook her head. "I think that was a decoy. I'm going with the theory someone wants to set up Mo. Since we have one of the largest gardens in Bay Isles, and everyone knows that, the mint was meant to point to her."

"I agree. I've never seen anyone out in our garden, especially a dead man," Henrietta said.

I thought about how Jim's fingers had been tinted green, and I knew he had clawed the ground before he died. But then I knew now where he died, and I had a theory how his murderer got him to the beach. More breaking and entering into backyards was in store for me today.

"We need to end this nonsense today or the police will shut down the café with their search warrant." Granny twisted a cloth napkin sitting in her lap. "What's next, an arrest?"

"They won't arrest me," I lied to keep Granny calm. "I didn't have a motive. And even though a lot of evidence points my way, they have to be wondering what would I have to gain by killing Jim?" The cops were getting to me and I knew it was only a matter of time before they arrested me.

"What was the murderer's motive?" Aurora asked.

"I have a few theories. Our Aunt Tammera's private investigator found out that Jim and Erica were not divorced, like Aurora suspected. Also, Jim's wealthy father, Donald, lived in Chicago and recently passed after a short illness. Jim and his older brother were the only heirs." I let that sink in while I took a sip of coffee. "The older brother hasn't been seen for years after he moved to Australia, and rumor had it that Jim's father had cut the older brother out of his will."

"Could it be the older brother is back in the picture?" Aurora asked. "If he killed off Jim, then he came back to town, he would be the only heir."

I nodded. "Or there's someone else who stands to gain."

"Was Jim's dad married?" Aurora asked.

"He was, but his second wife passed away a few years ago. She wasn't Jim's mom. She was his stepmom. Jim and his older brother's biological mom died when Jim was twelve." I glanced at my running watch.

"Did you remember the third thing Aunt Tammera said?" I asked Granny.

Granny shook her head. "Not yet. I'll call her later. I know you'll figure this all out."

I grinned at Granny and patted her hand. "We will." I wanted to calm everyone down. It had been pretty rough the last week in our sleepy village.

"You have a knack for these things," Aurora said, placing her cup in the sink and smiling at me sympathetically.

I nodded. "Let's meet at the café at noon. And don't forget to invite Deputy Drew," I added, hoping he was willing to listen to my theories. I rolled a muffin into a napkin and placed it on my backpack. I was zipping it up when Aurora walked over and handed me my cell.

"Don't forget your phone." She glanced at it. "You have 12 % battery now."

"Thanks." I slipped it into my backpack.

"Be careful," she whispered as she hugged my neck.

After I loaded Snickers into the golf cart, I told him to stay as I went in search for Jet.

My meeting with Jet confirmed what I already suspected. He had been nervous about what he'd done, but he apologized for selling some of our garden cuttings to a few of his friends without asking Granny first. That was one of the reasons he had lied when I had asked him the other
day about the gardens.

I checked my cell and read two texts, one from Missy at the Grille and one from Aunt Tammera. Both texts cemented my clues.

I was excited and nervous about my theory of the killer. Would it be enough to stick?

*Do you know how helpless you feel if you have a full
cup of coffee in your hand and you start to sneeze?*
~ Jean Kerr

CHAPTER TWENTY

The quaint neighborhood I had visited the night before looked quiet and safe in the late morning sun.

I hurried across the perfectly manicured front lawn of Felix's next-door neighbor's house. Clutching my backpack which held the pruning shears, I hoped I could sneak in the owner's backyard to cut off more evidence.

The broken gate swung open as easily as it had the night before. As I got closer to the garden, I slipped the mask over my mouth and put on the gloves. In the daylight, the colorful garden bloomed with an assortment of perennials and a neat row of herbs. My nose didn't even need to warn me, because in the middle of the garden, a foot off the gravel path, a large overrun patch of mint grew. I glanced behind me, and the shades to the house were drawn tight. I turned and knelt on the edge of the path, placing my backpack on the ground and removed the shears. I snipped off a few hearty twigs and placed them in a baggie.

I had placed the baggie in the sack and started to stand up, when I caught a glimpse of the shiny muzzle of a gun pointed at my head.

"Stand up slowly and turn around," said a menacing voice.

With a sweaty hand, I dropped the shears into my vest pocket. I stood up and turned slowly around.

"Well I'm not surprised to see you here," she said as she slowly waved the gun at me.

"You're not?" I gulped and stared at the barrel of gun that Kate Hawkins held. I wanted to confront her, but not now, and not like this. My fingers slid to the cold steel of the shears in my pocket wondering what kind of weapon they'd make.

"Can you lower your gun, so we can talk about this?" My heavy backpack threw me off balance a little, and I accidently stumbled.

Kate snorted. "Why should I?"

"Look I know how this may look. I thought I was in Jack's backyard. Sorry, I'll leave immediately, if you just lower your gun."

"You're lying. I knew it was you snooping around my backyard last night. Your sneezing gave you away. Too bad you dashed out of here.

I could have shot you, saying I'd mistaken you for a burglar." She shrugged. "Any case, I hear the police are about to arrest you."

"Arrest me?" I wanted to keep her talking. "You're the one who will need a lawyer," I said, sounding muffled through the cloth mask.

"Take off that mask. I want to see your mouth when you talk."

I took off the mask and immediately sneezed.

She laughed. I sneezed, and she laughed again.

"Let's move inside." Kate used the gun to motion me toward her patio and into the back door
that led to the kitchen.

With her free hand, Kate tugged on the sliding glass door that seemed stuck. Her other hand held the gun. She would need to put the gun down to use both of her hands. I thought about trying to stab her with the shears while she struggled with the sliding door. As if she read my thoughts, she quickly turned, leaving the sliding door slightly ajar.

Once inside, I had to stifle a gasp. Her kitchen made the Bridgeport Mount Trashmore county dump look like a country club. We were surrounded by precarious stacks of paper products of every imaginable kind – manila folders, crumbled papers, magazines, newspapers, and paperback books. Kate had weighed down the paper piles with clay pots filled with sprouting herbs. Messy piles of loose papers were spread out all over the kitchen table. The rest of the room was in shambles. Every inch of every surface was covered with stacks. It was hard to believe she would live like this.

"Now tell me what you're doing here," she snorted. "And no more lies."

For a few seconds, I was at a loss for words. I wondered how much evidence she knew the police had. "I came to ask you about Jim and your relationship with him."

"Me? Why do you think I knew him?"

I glanced around the kitchen, and in the hallway, I caught a glimpse of framed photos of seagulls, sunsets and palm trees. One particular photograph of the iconic Sydney Australia harbor bridge caught my eye.

"You've been seen together. And the police know this too." I had no idea what the police knew, but I had an idea that when Missy said Jim was seen with a dancer, that it could have been Kate Hawkins. She always wore yoga clothing, which could resemble a dance studio outfit. When I received the text from Missy saying that she remembered the lady with Jim drank the iced tea and lemonade combination, an Arnold Palmer, I knew it was Kate.

"So we travel in the same circles." She smirked.

I leaned against the kitchen table while she talked trying to look casual. But really my legs were about to buckle.

A slight breeze came through the open door and some papers rustled to the floor. I bent to pick them up, and when I did, I read the title of the document in my hand. It was a copy of a marriage certificate between Donald Grist and Melanie H. Racatelli. Aunt Tammera had told me Jim's dad was named Donald and Granny had said he married an Italian socialite from Chicago. Everything seemed to fall into place. Jim wasn't on a date with Kate at the Island Grille last week when they were seen together.

Holding the paper, I flipped it at Kate. "This is your relationship to Jim? He's your stepbrother? The "H" stands for Hawkins. Correct? Your mom's first late husband's name and your father's name."

"You really should mind your own business and stop snooping. You and your Granny think you know everything."

What did Granny know? Time to manipulate Kate's sense of arrogance. "That's right. We both know. You're crazy if you think you'd get away with another murder."

She shot me a look. "Murder?"

"Yes, it's an easy trail to follow, Kate. You thought if you poisoned Jim, you'd be in line for his father's inheritance. But then you found out he and Erica were still married, and she would have rights to his inheritance as his wife. You tried to kill her too."

"Neither Jim nor Erica deserve my mom's money." She waved the gun around. "Yes, my mom was married to his dad, and it killed her. Donald Grist killed her with his indiscretion. Jim's dad was a pig, just like Jim was. He drove my mom to drink, and eventually it killed her. They killed her."

I wondered if I didn't do something quick, I'd be shot. "So you thought by killing Jim and Erica, you'd be next in line? What about his older brother?"

She rolled her eyes up. "Oh, he's not coming back. Ever."

This sent a chill down my spine. I swallowed hard. I was playing with fire. "Did you kill him too?" I thought about the photo in her hallway of the Sydney harbor. Wasn't Australia the last known place for Jim's brother?

PAM MOLL

"You'll never know." She lifted the gun and pointed it in my direction.

"I know if you shoot me, you'll go to prison for a long time and never see that money. It will be hard for you to hide my body. Just like you tried to throw Jim's in the water that night. You don't know the tides, do you?"

"You think you know everything." Her eyes went wide.

"I know he didn't drown."

"He deserved to die. He was so mean and treated everyone like they were dirt. Just like his dad treated my mother." Kate sniffled. "I was sure the cyanide would work. I hoped it would cause confusion and I'd have time to get him to the boat. The poison would disappear from his system quickly, so after a few days in the Gulf there wouldn't be any trace of it and it would look like he was drunk and fell off his boat and drown."

"How'd you do it?"

"I lured him here to talk about his father's will. It was easy to put the poison in his third beer. We walked out back. He immediately became confused and started calling me names." She paused recalling that night.

I was glad for the distraction. I had to get her to let her guard down enough so I could go for the gun.

"Then Jim hit me. Enraged, I struck back and hurled myself at him. We both fell in the garden. He was bigger and a lot stronger than me, and maybe just as desperate." Kate wiped her free hand under her nose. "His knee to my stomach knocked the wind out of me. I gagged and struggled, and then suddenly he let go. He fell on all fours, his hands clutching the plants as he seemed to struggle for breath and then he died. The poison had done its work. I had to come up with another plan to get him to wash up on shore.

It happened so fast. I thought I would of had time to get him to sit in the canoe where he would slowly die while I paddled offshore away from the island."

Her words gave me chills. She was a psychopath. A pure, evil person. And I didn't doubt
for one minute that she would kill me too.

I kept my eyes locked on the muzzle of the gun while I felt the shears in my pocket. If only I could distract her for a second.

Suddenly, I heard the low rumble of a growl coming from behind Kate. I held my breath as Snickers slunk into the room with his teeth bared. Kate, having heard Snickers, spun around to point her gun at him.

Snickers must have had a sixth sense of what was happening. He didn't hesitate at all and charged forward and clamped his jaws around her leg. With her free leg, Kate viciously kicked at him. With a few whimpers, Snickers let go, and went down.

Enraged, I jumped toward her, intending to stab her with the shears. We both lost our balance and fell to the kitchen floor. The impact knocked the gun from her hand and it went flying across the floor. I knew I needed to act fast. But I'd never been in a fight, so my reactions were slow. Fortunately, my sidekick, Snickers knew what to do.

Snickers jumped up and started snapping at Kate's ankles as she tried to stand.

"Get off me!" Kate cursed and kicked.

I scrabbled across the floor, grabbed the gun and jumped up. "Stay still," I said, gasping for breath. I felt confident, until I saw Deputy Drew Powell standing at the doorway, gun drawn.

Drew looked at me sharply, then over at Kate. When he looked back at me his eyes were wary.

"Put the gun down, Molly," he shouted.

"It's not what you think." I put the gun carefully on the table and instinctively held my hands up in the air. "Wait a minute. It's Kate who should be in trouble here. She's the killer."

Shaking and kicking her feet at Snickers who was snarling with a mouthful of her pant leg, Kate yelled, "Thank goodness you're here, deputy. She and her dog attacked me! Arrest them!"

I opened my mouth to explain, but Drew surprised me when he pulled out his cuffs and instead of snapping them on me grabbed Kate's wrist.

His eyes met mine in a silent thank you as he put the handcuffs on her. "You're under arrest for the murder of James Grist and the attempted murder of Erica Alltop." He read Kate her rights after he secured the cuffs, and then called for back-up on his radio.

I was impressed that Mr. Handsome could multitask and was very relieved that the cuffs weren't going on my wrists.

I knelt down and hugged Snickers and buried my face in his neck. "Thank you." I whispered. "Good boy, I love you."

I wiped the tears from my eyes.

"Are you alright?" Drew asked me.

"Yeah. A little shaken up, but I'll be fine."

"Let's get you some fresh air."

Snickers squiggled out of my grasp, slurped his pink tongue up the side of my face, and scampered outside in search of a hedge.

Deputy Drew guided my shaky legs past Kate toward the back door. We stepped out on the porch. I looked back at Kate squirming faced down on the kitchen floor.

"You'll both pay for this," she yelled.

We stood in silence for a few seconds as we watched Snickers chase a squirrel up a tree by the mint garden.

We both laughed.

"It doesn't take too long to make everything better for a dog," I said.

"It doesn't take this cop very long to make everything better too." He crossed the patio and took me into a giant bear hug, released me, and looked me in the eye. "Mo, seriously, don't ever pull a stunt like this again, or I'll …"

"… You'll what? Arrest me?" I let out a nervous laugh.

"If that's what it takes to keep you safe. Promise?"

"Then I promise," I said, with my fingers crossed behind my back. "How'd you know I was here?"

"Aurora called me. She said she saw a text on your phone. Something about an Arnold Palmer, and she knew where you were headed."

I remembered Aurora handing me my phone, but I didn't realize she saw Missy's text. "But did you know why I came here?"

"Yes. I was coming to this conclusion with a lot of the same clues."

"And you knew I wasn't a killer all along?"

"My gut instincts told me what I needed to know. Besides, there's no way I would have wanted to kiss a killer."

I could feel my cheeks turn rosy. "You wanted to kiss me?"

"Yes. But you know, with law enforcement protocol and all …" His clear blue eyes shone.

I nodded and took a few steps back into the threshold of the kitchen and the patio.

His hands wrapped around my waist, sending sparks of desire shooting along my spine. Our eyes met, and I wasn't surprised at all when he kissed me. After all, we were standing under the mistletoe.

The kiss was sweet and exciting at the same time, exactly like I'd imagined kissing the man I'd fallen for would be.

The sound of sirens made us both step back. Within minutes, Deputy Ted Walker rushed through the back door. He looked at Kate on the floor and nodded at Drew.

"Great job," he said.

Was that directed toward me or Drew?

I caught a glimpse of myself in the mirror. My hair looked like I'd walked through a tornado and there were two thin black trails running down my cheeks where tears had made a mess of my mascara.

Within minutes, Detective Lacey sauntered into the kitchen. She bagged the gun and barely glanced my way. I knew I wasn't her biggest fan, but didn't she owe me an apology?

Instead she came up to me and said, "One could argue that I should arrest you for extreme stupidity."

I was about to open my mouth when she grinned.

Wow! A smile from the steel lady.

"Tell me this, Ms. Brewster. How'd you figure Kate got the body to the beach?" Lacey was surprisingly considerate. *Wow, she was asking me for a theory?*

"Well, do you remember the videotapes of the bridge that night?"

She nodded and chewed her puffy red lips.

"There's one vehicle early in the morning. I usually see it every day."

She motioned Drew and Ted over to listen to our discussion, while Detective Lacey's partner marched Kate out of the house.

"I'm not following you," Deputy Ted said.

"I knew from the start that it had to be a wheelbarrow of some type." I told them I thought I spotted two tire tracks in the sand before the tide washed them away. "I was so obsessed with the idea of a wheelbarrow or one of those beach carts, that I couldn't think of anything else." I thought about all the suspects garages and yards that I searched for wheelbarrows and mint gardens.

"Beach cart? "Detective Lacey asked.

"It's a wheelbarrow with two large, low pressure tires. They're designed so the wheels don't damage lawns or flower beds, and people here use
them to drag stuff to the beach," Drew said.

Lacey and Ted nodded.

"But when you mentioned that the victim had one of our napkins, it all seemed to click. At first I thought it was Felix or Jack Doughty."

"Why?" Ted asked.

"Because they own the Doughy Delight delivery truck that we see around the island. And it was spotted on that tape early in the morning before the bridge broke. It's common to see their pastry delivery truck."

They all nodded.

"You see, I heard a squeaky noise that night outside my window, and I couldn't place it. But then it all made sense about the napkin." I was so excited to tell my theory that I wasn't making sense.

"Slow down. Did Kate plant it?" Ted asked.

"No. Earlier that morning, Felix was at my shop and I collided with him, spilling my coffee on his work shirt. And come to think of it, Snickers slobbered on him too. He must have stuck the soiled napkins in his shirt pocket."

Drew shook his head. "But how did Kate get it?"

"When she stole her neighbor's truck." I grinned. "She poisoned Jim, and it acted so quick that he fell and rolled around in her garden. He clawed at the ground and grabbed a handful of the mint as he died. Her plan was to take him on the boat and dump him, so it would seem as if he had drowned. But instead, she panicked and snuck next door and used one of the tall metal pan cabinets from the truck to roll his body into. The heavy duty enclosed racks have wheels, making it easy to handle the daily deliveries to a restaurant, café or ..."

"... Doughnut shop," Ted finished.

"But a weak female like Kate would have had to tip it toward her to keep the body flat inside, leaving the front wheels up in the air in order to roll it on the boardwalk and to the beach."

"That's what caused the two tire marks?" Drew asked.

"Yes. And the back of the rack has a removable door," I said.

"A doughnut dolly used for the dearly departed," Ted commented with a grin.

"And in case anyone saw her, she wore the Doughy Doughnuts' work shirt left in Felix's truck, and somehow in that process, the soiled napkin in his pocket fell out and stuck to Jim's Velcro fishing vest." I recalled how Felix said he had another shirt he could wear. He must have left the soiled one in his truck.

"Is Felix an accomplice? How did she steal the truck without the keys?" Drew asked.

"No, they weren't accomplices. Felix and his cousin were at a holiday party that night in Holly Ridge, two towns past Bay Isles, just over the Palma County line, and yet far enough from here that they didn't want to drive home. They had phoned Kate to tell her they were spending the night at a friend's house and asked her to let out their dogs. She has a key to their house." I had stopped by Doughy Delights a few days ago to get their alibi. They told me they had a next-door neighbor that could vouch that they weren't home that night. I had no idea at the time who their neighbor was until a few days later. I felt bad not telling Drew everything I'd learned, but I couldn't risk confusing him with my theories any more than they already were.

"After Jim bit the dust, she went to their house and grabbed the keys to the pastry truck," Drew said, with a long sigh.

Was that admiration I just saw in Detective Lacey's eyes? No, my bad. It looked more like jealousy. She made a few notes on her pad. "When did you know this? Why didn't you tell us yesterday? You were withholding information in a criminal case."

"It all came together this morning. I knew when I confirmed that Kate lived next door to Felix, and when Missy, the bartender at the Grille, texted me and said the lady meeting with Jim drank Arnold Palmers."

Subconsciously, I think I had suspected she was involved from the day of the murder when Aurora mistakenly handed me a pink elastic hair tie thinking it was mine. It matched Kate's Bazooka-colored tennis shoes she often wore. I wore colorful elastic hair ties too, but the one found on the beach was a bright pink, which was an important clue.

Deputy Ted patted me on the back. "Well, Red, if you ever want a job on the police force, we could use a consultant like you."

Detective Lacey blushed but nodded at his comment.

I'll take that, I thought, my head still buzzing from adrenaline and Deputy Handsome's kiss.

My best weekend plans usually involve good coffee,
comfort foods, and stretchy pants.
~ Nanea Hoffman

CHAPTER TWENTY-ONE

When the dust settled, and the police crime tapes were removed, there was no place like my café.

Granny Dee and Aurora met me at the back door. We exchanged hugs, and from the tight squeezes I knew that the news had traveled fast.

"If you ever do something like that again," Granny said, "I'm not sure my heart can handle it. Dear Lord, if you had been shot … don't you ever go after a crazy woman holding a loaded gun again!" She paused and added, "Unless you have a gun too."

"I didn't know she was home. I only wanted
to get a sample of her mint …," I stopped talking. "Oh, never mind. It all worked out. And I promise to stay out of trouble for a while."

Granny leaned over and gave me a peck on the cheek. "I hope not."

"Come on. Let's get you a coffee. Everyone's here," Aurora said.

"Everyone?" I asked.

Aurora put her arm around my shoulders and smiled even broader as we walked into the café from the kitchen. It was filled with my work family and friends, all gathered around the tables. They all quieted, eyes filled with expectation.

Aurora took my hand and held it over my head, like I was a prize fighter who won a major boxing bout. "She did it!" she exclaimed.

I smiled in delight when the café broke out into an applause and cheering. The clapping intensified when Snickers came to stand by me, like

it was meant for him.

"Thank you all for being here today. Your support of this café and this community is awesome," I said, with a lump in my throat.

"And we will sleep a little safer at night knowing the killer is behind bars, thanks to you," Bales said.

I nodded at a loss for words. I felt a rush of happiness.

One of Jim's fishing buddies and the mayor's son both came forward and shook my hand.

I hugged my barista, Chris, and he whispered, "I never believed the rumors that you were the main suspect."

"Thank you," I whispered back.

"Did you hear Erica is getting released from the hospital tomorrow, just in time for her mother to arrive home to take care of her?" Aurora said. I was always amazed that Aurora had her finger on

everything going on in Bay Isles.

"That's great. I'm so happy she'll be okay," I said, shivering with excitement. I felt blessed that everyone was safe, and no one else had been murdered … and that no one in my family had been arrested. It felt great to know the person responsible for one death and an assault would be behind bars for a long time.

"Oh, and Mo," Granny said.

"What?" I turned toward her.

"I remembered what Aunt Tammera said to me." A furrow appeared between her gray eyebrows, and I figured it was important for her to finally tell me, even after the fact the case had been solved.

All eyes turned to Granny Dee.

"The information," she said.

274

"Well?" I asked.

"The third thing she said was that his stepsister had moved to Florida. She didn't give me

details, but I assumed it had to do with the case."

I blinked. "Thanks Granny." And then I laughed and hugged her shoulder. "It is all connected."

"Nice detective work, Mo," Granny Dee said. "Now let's talk about how you knew."

Me, Granny, Aurora, Bales, Chris and the lawyer who Deputy Drew had sent over, DC, were all gathered around a table. By the time I went through all the details of the clues, like I had with the detectives and officers, it was late in the afternoon.

We laughed and relaxed, and I felt so at home with my odd little group.

"So where do you think Kate got the poison?" Bales asked.

"It could have been used for industrial purposes," DC said. "Kate knew what she was doing. It was a premeditated murder. I suppose she tried to kill him first and then dump his body in the water to make any diagnosis difficult, so it would look like a drowning. Had Molly not found his body, the high tides that were coming in that morning might have eventually drifted him out to sea. I'm sure we'll know soon enough," he concluded.

"If Mo hadn't found everything out, she could be in jail and the café could have been shut down," Bales said.

"Will the police charge Felix or Jack Doughty from Doughy Delights with anything?" Aurora asked DC.

"Not if they are above board, like they said," DC assured, smiling broadly. I think all his smiles had a lot to do with the spiked hot cocoa Chris had given him.

"More importantly is that Kate broke down and spilled everything about committing the crimes," I said. "Poor Erica, to be caught up in this mess." I shook my head. "It's hard to believe Kate would lose her head over an inheritance, even a big one like Jim's dad left."

"Well, in her case she had another rationalization for getting rid of Jim, and possibly his brother, because she felt they killed her mother."

"Or she thought she was doing the world a favor by getting rid of horrid person," Aurora mumbled.

A few of my baristas nodded.

"But Kate's lawyers can still screw things up in court," Granny said. "No offense," she added looking at DC.

"No offense taken. Kate did give everyone here a few scary days, but there seems to be enough evidence pointed at her, and a solid motive. Her inheritance will be in question too," DC said.

"I wouldn't be surprised if that officer friend of yours, Drew Powell, does receive a promotion to Detective after solving the murder case so quickly." Granny rubbed her hands together.

"It is Christmastime. A time for new beginnings." I thought about Deputy Drew. His kiss still lingered on my lips and in my brain. Now that I wasn't a murder suspect, I wondered if dating was a possibility. Turns out, that's a biggie when it comes to determining if a relationship with an officer is on the horizon.

"To new beginnings." Granny Dee held up her tea cup.

Everyone held up their coffee cups.

"To new beginnings and happy endings," I said.

Everyone cheered and chuckled.

Christmas Eve

EPILOGUE

A few weeks later, Granny, with my strong insistence, had decided to throw a small party at her house. After all, it had turned out to be a wonderful Holly Fest and Jim's murder was solved.

It wasn't often Granny opened her home, but we had a lot to celebrate. Usually her anti-yuletide sentiments could sour the best eggnog.

The doorbell rang. Snickers jumped up and barked his warning. Roco didn't even raise his cute mug face. George, in his Siamese cat style, snoozed comfortably under the coffee table with Bullet, mom's cat, nearby. Thank heavens the two cats had made a connection.

I stood in the foyer, taking it all in. It was adjacent to the living room where everyone would soon be gathered. The wall furthest from me was lined up with long card tables covered with red and green linen cloths. On each of the tables, highly polished silver serving dishes reflected the glow of the fire burning in the fireplace. The trays were layered with appetizers and scrumptious-looking desserts and pastries. Henrietta had pulled out all the stops. She had been polishing silver and preparing food for days.

Swinging open the door to the front porch, I saw the faces of my friends and our guests gathered.

"Merry Christmas, all," I said, opening the berry-wreath-cladded door wide. "Go on in. Granny's waiting in the living room. My mom, Henrietta, and Jet are there too."

One by one, they passed me as I greeted them, and we exchanged hugs. "Glad you all could join us," I said as my baristas Aurora, Bales, and Chris showed up. Fiona came in next, helping Erica, who was healing quickly from her injuries. She had a few memory lapses, but the doctor had assured her   the concussion wasn't permanent. Erica had made a full recovery a week ago and would be able to testify against Kate Hawkins.

"I'm so glad you're feeling better," I said, giving Erica a sympathetic, but loving, look. I closed the door as we gathered in the foyer.

"Again, thank you for finding me when you did," Erica said, her hand reaching for mine and squeezing it.

I nodded, trying to fight back tears.

Fiona stood watching as Erica made her way to the living room. She handed me an envelope. "Merry Christmas, Mo."

"Thank you. I love getting Christmas cards. You're so kind."

"There's a little something for you and your café in there. You did so much for Erica while I was

away, and we can't thank you enough."

"No, Fiona." I gave the red envelope back to her. "I can't take it." I had heard that Erica had benefited financially from Jim's dad's will. Their divorce hadn't been final, and she was now the only heir of the estate. It was sad to think there were no other family member left. I may have a quirky family, but I still had my mom, Granny, my brother and his family, and a handful of crazy aunts. I'll spill more about my aunties one day.

"Please, we insist." Fiona glanced toward Erica. She looked our way, smiled, and nodded. "Besides, you'll need to find a new barista."

"What?" I feigned surprise. I knew Fiona was quitting, and that she and Erica's father were getting back together.

"I'm sure you heard," Fiona grinned.

"So, it's true? I'm so happy for you and your

family."

Her shoulders relaxed, and before she could reply the doorbell rang again.

"We'll catch up later, dear. Tend to your guests," Fiona said, making her way to the living room.

Mayor Clawson, his wife Trudy, and his son Todd came in, trailed by the mayor's brother DC, who was now officially my new lawyer.

DC had let his snow-white beard grow out. And for the occasion, he was dressed in a red Santa suit and a matching hat.

"DC, how appropriate," I giggled. "You look just like him."

"I have to be at the Children's hospital later. I just stopped by to say hello," he said. His round-as-a-dinner-plate face was flushed red. "Ho, ho, ho!"

"Welcome Santa Clawson. Come on in."

Our small group laughed and drank, and for the most part stayed away from the murder case discussions. I had invited Deputy Drew and Ted, but this was a busy time of the year for them, and they had replied that they weren't sure they would make it. After all, they were making their rounds at all the charity events, and still had our sleepy village to protect.

Aurora looked like she had died and gone to heaven. I watched as she and Todd Clawson sat laughing in the corner.

Twenty minutes later, the doorbell rang again.

I opened the door to a smiling Drew. He was tanned, lean and nicely filled out his green sweater worn over a checked shirt and tan trousers. His green eyes shone under his long lashes.

I felt a brief blush cross over my cheeks when I realized Drew and I were dressed in the same shades of green. I blushed because I pictured us in our coordinating outfits on a Christmas card.

I wore a little vintage green velvet dress with a lace collar and cuffs. If I added a red scarf, I'd pass for one of Santa's elves. It had been an unusually cooler night, and I wore a soft, cast-off sweater of my mother's over the dress.

Speaking of my mother, she was sitting on the couch next to Henrietta, and across from Granny. She and Granny eyed me and Drew standing in the foyer with curiosity.

"You look gorgeous," he said, and his eyes lit up as he smiled at me.

"Thank you. You do too."

"What's this?" I asked, as he handed me a foiled wrapped pie tin.

282

"Peppermint pie," he smiled brightly.

"What!" I murmured incredulously.

"Just kidding. It's mincemeat pie. Ted's wife made it and sent it over."

Oh, I loved that smile. It could melt ice cream on a cold day.

"Well, tell him thank you."

"I will. It's nice to see everyone gathered around in Granny's living room."

Henrietta and Jet had joined the Christmas Eve celebration, and when Drew eyed them in the corner talking, he turned to me and asked, "When did you know it was Jet who sold the mint plant clippings to Kate?"

"I wasn't sure who he sold them to. I did know that Kate had said she and Jet hung out, which I found a bit odd. And when I confronted Jet, he lied, only because he was afraid he hadn't asked permission from Granny Dee to sell her herb clippings."

He nodded and bent low, and whispered in my ear, "You are truly amazing."

Granny and my mom whispered from across the room.

Noticing them, Drew straightened up. "The

house looks so festive." It seemed a flicker marred Drew's impish grin for a moment, but then thankfully, it was back to full wattage.

"What makes it so special are the friends and family gathered around enjoying the holiday spirit. By the way, there are tons of appetizers, if you're hungry. And for drinks we have hot cocoa, champagne, and spiked eggnog."

"I'll stick to the cocoa," he said, and smiled. "You never know when I'll get a call. And hopefully it's never going to be about another body on the beach."

"Never say never," I smiled.

We stood a few seconds in the foyer listening to Christmas music in the background before the Mayor called him over.

Drew and I walked over to the Mayor Clawson and his wife.

I felt a little awkward considering my brief history with Drew … and umm … well the circumstances that had brought us together.

Drew confirmed to everyone gathered around that Jim, the vic, as he called him, had an older brother, and that the two had always had a rivalry of sorts. Jim was the black sheep, while his brother could do no wrong. His brother had a falling out with his stepmother, Kate's mom, and he went to live in Australia. They grew apart, and when he didn't come home when his stepmom got ill and passed, his father became estranged from him. And then when his father became ill, and the eldest son didn't return to the U.S. He was removed from the will.

"That's terrible," Granny mumbled.

"The thing is, Jim's brother couldn't return home. He had gone missing years ago. And I uncovered during the timeline that he had stopped all correspondence. This coincided with a trip Kate made to Australia. His body was never found, but foul play was always suspected."

Mayor Clawson said to Erica, "Kate was one cold b ..." he paused, looked at Granny, and finished with "... fish." He shook his head. "I still can't believe she poisoned Jim and then conked you on the head like that."

"Kate did this because of greed," Drew said. "She was messed up. Greed and jealousy pushed her to murder. She had always been jealous of her stepdad's love for his sons. And in the end, she wanted revenge that he had been unfaithful to her mother ..."

"... and the inheritance," Erica interjected in a soft voice. "She wanted the money."

"Yes. Money is strong motivation," Drew said, nodding at Erica. "Because of her name changes and aliases, it was hard to track down her history."

I'll have to ask Aunt Tammera about her private investigator friend's sources one day, I thought. *He found information on Kate before the authorities had.*

"Turns out that growing prized herbs was a strong clue." He smiled at me. "The mocha mentha piperia herb … ah, … peppermint … and the oils it contained, especially the menthol and menthone, were not in his digestive tract and were only found on his body, mainly on his hands. And it may have taken us days to analyze it, but Mo knew right away."

I smiled and blushed beneath my makeup. "You would have found out soon enough," I shot back.

A few heads nodded. The room was silent until my mom entered from the kitchen, humming tunelessly as she carried a double-layered birthday cake. Henrietta trailed her with a stack of paper
plates and a serving knife.

"It's my famous chocolate cake with a coffee-spiked crème anglaise sauce swirled over mocha icing," Henrietta beamed.

"That's fabulous, Henrietta! I love it." And I did love the cake. "You must have been baking all day. Thank you." I gave her a hug.

Granny harrumphed at the coffee-flavored cake. Timothy Carlin now seated next to Granny, patted her hand.

"There's a pineapple-upside-down cake for you, Dee, and anyone else who doesn't like chocolate cake with coffee icing," Henrietta offered.

Timothy lit the large number 3 and 0 candles and everyone sang Happy Birthday to me, while I blushed the entire time.

"Thanks, um, thank you all," I murmured awkwardly.

"It's time for a toast," the Mayor said, breaking the silence.

Henrietta refilled our flute glasses from bottles of premium champagne, which fizzed merrily as we all held them up for a toast.

"A toast to Deputy Drew. He was able to get a confession from Kate on where to locate Jim's brother's body," Mayor Clawson chimed.

Ooohs and aaahs filled the room, and everyone drank a toast, and then clapped.

"And if I could, I'd like to consider the birthday girl, Mo, as an honorary mayor of Bay Isles for the day. Thank you." Mayor Clawson said and held up his glass.

My mind spun out the fantasy for a few seconds, and then I said, "I couldn't have done it without all your help." I paused, and added, "and, of course, Snickers."

Snickers barked. Everyone laughed.

I made eye contact with Deputy Drew and winked at him. He raised his glass and gave me a wonderful smile.

After making the rounds and talking with all our guests, I stepped outside on the back patio.

A few seconds later, Drew followed me.

"Beautiful evening," he said, standing very close.

And it was.

"How can I repay you?" Drew asked with a boyish grin.

A dozen ideas raced through my mind, but I settled on one. "A proper date would be nice."

"It's a deal," he replied immediately. "We should seal a vow like that with a kiss, don't you think?"

Before I could answer yes, his hands were in my hair and the kiss he planted on my lips was soft. The one I returned became urgent and seeking. It was equally met.

He gave me a comical wince, and I poked at his arm playfully.

Drew was about to kiss me again, when Snickers barked at the door and it sent us both backward in an attempt to put space between us.

"We better return to the party," I said.

He nodded, and his shoulders slumped a bit.

"Are you available to come by the café tomorrow to fix the tile?" I asked playfully.

"The tile?" He grinned. "But it's Christmas day."

"Exactly."

He nodded, and we went back inside. I looked around the room and tried to take it all in. Over the past few weeks I had gotten to know my Bay Isles family and neighbors like I never expected.

"Granny, how are you doing?" I whispered.

"My dear Miss Molly, I don't think I'll ever have an exciting holiday season as much as I did this year. It was like I was living in an Agatha Christie novel."

I wasn't Hercule Poirot, but I did follow a persistent hunch that solved the murder case. It inspired me to announce, "To quote Poirot, I'd have to say: 'I have the honor to retire from the case ...'" I grinned at Granny, Mom and Drew.

RECIPE COFFEE BREAK

Granny's Note: Do NOT include Cyanide

Sweet and Salty Peppermint – Pretzel Bark

You can make large batches without pans or a refrigerator!

Makes 12 Servings

½ tsp. peppermint extract

1 cup coarsely chopped pretzel sticks

(16-oz.) package vanilla candy coating chopped

1/3 cup coarsely chopped peppermint candy canes

Parchment paper

1. Microwave vanilla candy coating in a 1 qt. microwave-safe bowl at Medium (50% power) 1 minute; stir. Microwave until melted and smooth,

stirring at 30-second intervals. Stir in peppermint extract.

2. Spread half of melted candy coating about 1/8-inch-thick in a parchment paper-lined jelly-roll pan. Sprinkle ½ cup chopped pretzels and 1/3 cup chopped candy canes over melted candy coating, and press into coating. Repeat with remaining ingredients on another parchment paper-lined jelly-roll pan. Chill 5 minutes or until cool and firm. Note: We used Loghouse Candiquick Vanilla Candy Coating and Neisen-Massey Pure Peppermint Extract.

Make even larger quantities for gifting this easy treat by skipping the jelly-roll pan and covering your counter with parchment. It'll take longer to harden at room temperature.

Peppermint Oreo Popcorn Bark

Popcorn and Oreos, this was a favorite snack of my kids. This no-bake treat makes for a great holiday gift. Can be made with white or milk chocolate. For a more festive feel, add sprinkles.

Makes a few pounds.

- 16 Oreo Cookies
- 30 Starlight Peppermint Candies
- 2 Bags No Butter Microwave popcorn (lightly salted)
- Bag of Chocolate (I used Candiquik, it melts well, I've also used Ghirardelli chips.)
- Sprinkles (optional)

PEPPERMINT MOCHA MURDER

1. Line a cookie sheet with a wax paper.

2. Pop the microwave popcorn (pull out any un-popped kernels)

3. In ziplock bags (use one for each) crush peppermint and Oreo (You can use a kitchen mallet to crush them.)

4. Melt chocolate according to the instructions on the package.

5. In a large bowl, mix popcorn, peppermints and Oreos. Mix in 2/3 of chocolate.

6. Pour mixture onto the wax paper and spread out. Drizzle remaining 1/3 of chocolate on top of mixture and top with sprinkles.

7. Place in refrigerator for 10 minutes and break into pieces.

8. Serve and enjoy!

Granny D's Gooey Butter Cake

Molly's favorite family tradition

Makes 24 Servings

---

1 package of yellow
    cake mix

3 eggs

½ cup melted butter

8 oz. cream cheese

3 Cups Powdered
    Sugar

1. Preheat oven to
    350 degrees.

2. Mix cake mix,
    melted butter
    and one egg
    together.

3. Pat firm mixture into a 9x13 greased metal cake pan. (Granny tried a glass pan but please note, that you should reduce baking temperature by 25 degrees and check the cake often as it may be ready up to ten minutes earlier if you are substituting a glass pan for a metal baking pan. This is because glass doesn't heat up as quickly as metal but will become very hot once heated up.)

4. Mix cream cheese, 2 ¾ cups powdered sugar and 2 eggs together until smooth. Don't over beat. Spread mixture on top of cake base.

5. Bake at 350 degrees for 30-40 minutes.

6. Let cool 15 minutes, sprinkle ¼ cup powdered sugar on top of cake. Let cool completely.

7. Cut into squares.

Candy Cane Fudge

If you like red velvet cake, you'll love Granny's favorite fudge.

Makes 3 lbs.

---

1 tsp. butter

2/3 cup semisweet chocolate chips

3 tsp. shortening, divided

2 pkg. (12 oz.) white baking chips, divided

1 can (14 oz.) sweetened condensed milk

1 ½ tsp. red paste food coloring

4 cups powdered sugar, divided

6 oz. cream cheese softened

¼ tsp. peppermint extract

1 tsp. vanilla extract

3 Tbs. crushed peppermint candies

1. Line a 13x9 in. pan with foil; grease foil with butter. (If you like, you can spoon the mixture into paper-lined

mini-muffin cups instead of
spreading it into a pan,)

2. In a large microwave-safe bowl,
    combine 3 ¼ cups white baking
    chips, chocolate chips and 2 tsp.
    shortening. Microwave, uncovered,
    on high for 1 minute; stir. Microwave
    at additional 15-second intervals,
    stirring until smooth. Stir in
    sweetened condensed milk and food
    coloring; gradually add 1 cup
    powdered sugar. Spread in prepared
    pan.

3. In another large microwave-safe
    bowl, melt remaining white baking
    chips and shortening; stir until
    smooth. Beat in cream cheese and
    peppermint and vanilla extracts.
    Gradually beat in remaining
    powdered sugar until smooth.
    Spread over red layer; sprinkle with
    crushed candies. Refrigerate two
    hours or until firm.

PAM MOLL

4. Using foil, lift fudge out of pan.
   Remove foil; cut fudge into 1 in.
   squares. Store between layers of
   waxed paper in an airtight container.

ABOUT THE AUTHOR

PAM MOLL

Pam Moll loves traveling and attributes her creative inspiration to it. Many of her adventures are to remote tropical islands. She lives on an island near Saint Petersburg, Florida. Pam has published several catalogs, calendars, guide books, and novels.

I hope you enjoyed Book One of the Molly Brewster Mystery Series! Your feedback is important to me and inspires me.

If you liked Book One: *Peppermint Mocha Murder*, please go to www.gopamela.com and register to be the first to receive Book 2 in the series: *Boats, Bunnies and Bodies*. Get on the list to Pre-Order Book 3 and 4 and win an Amazon Gift Card: www.gopamela.com

In the meantime, if you liked this and other stories by Pam, please go to where you bought it, and write a review, so other readers can hear from you.

Or leave a review on Goodreads or Amazon. Thanks for reading!

BOOKS by Pam Moll

Plush
Island of Lies
Girl Alone on an Island
Diamond Island
Peppermint Mocha Murder
Boats, Bunnies and Bodies ~ Coming Soon
SUE ME   A retread of Plush

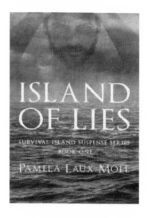

Two survivors. One island. No one to trust...

Ryleigh Lane desperately needed a vacation. The whistle-blower is about to appear in court to go up against a corrupt pharmaceutical exec. If she's successful, the case will reveal a deadly secret. Shortly before the trial, a carefree cruise with her new boyfriend, Elliot, changes everything. A sudden storm leaves them stranded alone on a tiny island.

Elliot Finn is incredibly mysterious... and completely sexy. His resourcefulness helps Ryleigh get through the early days on the island. But as they fight for survival, Ryleigh realizes they're both guarding dark secrets.

Romance blooms alongside suspicion. Will this new case put Ryleigh's life on the line?

Island of Lies is the first book in the Survival Island series, a set of suspenseful thriller novels. If you like sizzling chemistry, riveting suspense, and twists you won't see coming, then you'll love Pamela Laux Moll's captivating series starter.

Buy *Island of Lies* to journey to the island today!

A deadly paradise. A family secret. Fighting for her life could mean saving thousands more...

On the day Ryleigh Lane became stranded on a tropical island, she hadn't spoken to her twin sister Cally for 10 years, and she never will again if she can't get home.

Missing for over a month, Ryleigh must continue to survive the sun-filled days and terrifying nights. As the hours tick away, she wonders how soon it will be until the island tremors and treasure hunters end her life.

Surrounded by massive rodents and poisonous snakes, Ryleigh has no choice but to get off the island. But before that can happen, there's just one more thing she needs to accomplish...

Girl Alone on an Island is the second book in the exhilarating Survival Island series. If you like fast-paced action, gripping suspense, and captivating plot twists, then you'll love Pamela Laux Moll's nail-biting novel.

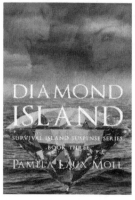

PAM MOLL

Diamond Island

A forgotten treasure. An ill-fated island. Twin sisters are hot on the trail of a multi-generational mystery…

After being stranded for a month on a deserted island, Ryleigh Lane is home safe. But she'd rather be back on the island. She knows her temporary tropical home holds the key to uncovering an incredible family secret. She'll stop at nothing to find out the truth, but her rich and ruthless nemesis is just as determined to find the Lane fortune first. Even if it means disposing of its rightful heiress.

Stalked by enemies at every turn, Ryleigh enlists her twin sister and their CIA agent boyfriends for help. They embark upon a wild hunt for clues from South Florida to the South Pacific.

With immense riches on the line, it's impossible to know who to trust. Can Ryleigh uncover the treasure and the truth… before she too is buried deep beneath the sand?

Diamond Island is the third book in the Survival Island saga, a series of sea adventure novels that mix the action of Clive Cussler with the romance of Nora Roberts. If you like vivid tropical settings, pulse-pounding plot twists, and passion on the high seas, then you'll love Pamela Laux Moll's steamy thrillers.

Buy *Diamond Island* to return to a dangerous paradise today!

52641024R00190

Made in the USA
Columbia, SC
11 March 2019